THE INHERITANCE

THE INHERITANCE

Clyde Skaggs

Clyde Skaggs

Minuteman Press
Liverpool, New York

PUBLISHED BY CWS ENTERPRISES
4023 Brixham Ct., Baldwinsville, NY 13027

Cover design; cover photographs, and book design by Clyde Skaggs.
4023 Brixham Court,
Baldwinsville, NY 13027

ISBN 0-9743003-1-4

Manufactured in the United States of America.
May 2004

FOR JESSIE

Acknowledgements

There are a number of people to whom I would like to give special thanks for their contribution to the creation of this novel.

I want to thank my brother, Frank Skaggs, whose knowledge and experience helped me formulate the basis for this story. I owe a very special thank-you to my editor, Kathleen Brown, for her generous and unselfish effort. I'm grateful to my granddaughter, Jessica Zegarelli, for encouraging me to write, and to my grandson, Jonathan Zegarelli, for his assistance with computer searches. I owe a debt of gratitude to the Syracuse Roundtable Writer's Group, for their critique and feedback and to my fellow writer, Cornelius Hayes, for his encouraging me to publish. My appreciation goes to Dan Schmidt and Patti Cramer, at Merrill Lynch for their financial and tax advice, Dr. Nabil Aziz, for the neurological information I received through his office, and to the nursing staff of the intensive care unit at Crouse Hospital for the information they provided. Thanks to Laurence Kuhn, at Minuteman Press for his guidance on printing requirements, Dave Hudson, for his advice on corporate business practices, and Carol Mounce, for her contribution to preparation of the book cover.

And most of all, I want to thank my wife, Jessie, for her continuous patience, understanding, and helpful suggestions during the entire process of writing this novel.

THE INHERITANCE

PROLOGUE

It was dark in the alley, but there was a street light at the entrance behind him. He could see the reflections of that light as tiny firefly-like specks from what he knew were the headlights of the car that was waiting for him. This is a stupid idea, he thought as he started down the alley. Even though he was wired and had prearranged for back up, he knew he was taking a chance.

His size, being outlined in front of the light, would give them a big advantage. He was counting on past yearlong dealings with the drug gang leading up to tonight's big deal to cause them to be confident that he was on the level. If so, he would have enough advantage to pull it off.

He made sure his gun was where he could get it quickly, wiped his hand across his red beard, pulled his pants upward with his elbows and started ahead. Sweeping the alley with his eyes as he moved forward, he could hear only an occasional car go past the entrance and see minimal lights from windows in the alley since they were in a fast deteriorating neighborhood almost void of inhabitants. They knew how to pick their spots he thought. Just like they had in the past. He had, for the last year, allowed them to choose the location of their transactions in order to build up their confidence in his being a legitimate buyer. Unlike normal drug traffickers dealing in cocaine or heroine, these dealers specialized in less lethal and less potent drugs, but actually more dangerous, because the drugs were aimed specifically at young people. Ecstasy, amphetamines, and crack had become more prolific and preferred amongst high school and younger kids during recent years. Therefore, if he couldn't get out of vice, and had to take extra chances, it would be for something that counted; to stop drug dealers that kill kids.

Then they opened fire.

He didn't see the car speed by him. Neither did he see the back-up arrive too late to be of any help.

When Detective Lieutenant Ethan Williams woke up, he was in the hospital.

CHAPTER ONE

Ethan sat waiting, his two hundred twenty pound, six foot frame, looking cramped by the armchair in which he was sitting. He was nervous. He ran his fingers through his red hair and crossed his large muscular legs. In a moment, just as he had uncrossed them, the office door opened. The man who entered was tall skinny, had a slight paunch, wore wire-rimmed glasses and had thinning neatly combed gray hair. Ethan's heart rate increased and he took a deep breath.

"Good morning, Ethan," he said.

"Good morning, Captain."

Walking around to sit at his desk, Ethan's boss said, "What's up?"

"I'm here to tell you I quit."

"You can't . . ." Captain Ross started to say.

Ethan held up his hand palm out, and said, "Hold it! Don't start again with the speech. I've asked you how many times to get me out of Vice? Ten? Fifty? A hundred? Too many to count! And what has it gotten me? Promises, Innuendos, excuses, and I don't know what else. Well, that's it! I want out!" He walked over to the desk that looked large compared to the scrawny captain sitting behind it. Ethan looked at him defiantly, laid his badge and gun not to gently on the desk and turned his back, while hesitating slightly before starting for the door. He knew he had already made the decision to start his own PI business, but couldn't help having some remorse about leaving the Syracuse Police Department after eight years. Ethan was only thirty-two years old and wondered if he might be acting rashly. He had spent the entire eight years in Vice. and was good at the job but tired of dealing with the scum of the earth. Too much of the work was undercover, making him feel like he was part of the problem instead of the solution. He liked to be clean-shaven and reasonably well dressed. Most of the time, the job didn't allow this, nor did it allow him to keep the reasonable hours most humans worked each week.

After leaving the office, he decided to go for a long walk to relax and then to the courthouse to register the Ethan Williams Investigations business.

"Good morning," the elderly, gray-haired clerk said, as Ethan approached the counter on the second floor of the courthouse. "What can I do for you?"
"I'd like to file a DBA."
"Under what name?"

4

"Ethan Williams Investigations."

"Write it down for me." The clerk instructed.   "You can fill this out while I run the name through the system." No new business could be registered until it was determined that there was no other business of the same name registered in the county. The clerk came back, took the completed form, and gave Ethan two notarized copies.

"That'll be thirty dollars please.   Good luck, Mr. Williams."

Elizabeth Jordon, Beth to her friends, had been lying in bed looking at the ceiling. She was unable to sleep. All kinds of things were going through her head. Ethan wanted her to move to Syracuse, and she didn't want to go. She loved him very much but wasn't sure they could get together because of the issue of who should move.

"Oh, shit," she said jumping out of bed and grabbing the clock from the nightstand with both hands. She had forgotten to set the alarm. It was seven-ten in the morning already. She thought, I'll never make it by eight o'clock. Well, I'll just be late. Her lieutenant had told her the night before to be in his office at eight o'clock sharp. He didn't say why, but it was probably another shitty assignment.

Setting the clock, which now read seven-fifteen, back on the nightstand, she hurried into the bathroom. She looked into the mirror and seeing that her long, wavy, red hair was a mass of tangles, grabbed a brush from alongside the sink and started brushing briskly in spite of the pain caused by the tangles. After doing what she could with her hair, she turned on the hot water faucet and rested her face in her hands while waiting for the water to get hot. Picking up the washcloth from the counter, she soaked it in hot water, and wiped her face and neck. The hot water felt wonderful. She stepped into the closet and pulled on a pair of blue slacks and a white blouse. Grabbing a gray blazer from the rack, she headed for the kitchen. While pouring herself a glass of juice, she realized, coffee would have to wait until she got to the office.

The traffic was terrible because it had snowed again the previous night. Baltimore Department of Public Works failed miserably when it came to handling snow. It really bugged Elizabeth because she had moved to Baltimore from Syracuse where they handled snow like Californians handled sunshine.

It was almost eight-thirty when Beth arrived at police headquarters, and she went straight to Lieutenant Chuck Jones' office and knocked on the closed door.

"Come in," a voice said.

She opened the door and before being completely inside, said to the thin black man behind the desk, "Chuck, I'm sorry for being so late, but I overslept, and the damn snow didn't help much either."

"Don't worry about it. Have you had coffee?"

"No."

"Well, go get some and come right back."

While she was gone, Chuck picked up the phone and dialed an intercom number. "Hi, Captain. This is Chuck. She's here and is out getting coffee."

"Okay, I'll be right there."

When Elizabeth was back in the office and seated, she said, "What's up?" and then took a sip of her coffee.

"Beth, I've got a surprise for you."

The last time she heard that, she had been sent to a hellhole in New York State for two days to bring a suspect back, and it lasted a week. Because it was out of town, he acted like it was a damn vacation. A knock on the door brought her out of her reverie.

"Come in," Chuck said.

As the captain entered, Beth stood quickly. "Good morning, Captain."

"Good morning," he said. "Detective Jordon, you've been doing a terrific job. We received a report from the Syracuse Police last year concerning your help there which contributed heavily to your earning a promotion."

He reached into the right hand pocket of his gray tweed jacket and pulled out a shiny badge. "Detective, it gives me great pleasure to present this Lieutenant's badge to you." He handed her the badge, and extended his hand saying, "Congratulations, Lieutenant Jordon."

Grinning, she accepted the badge, shook his hand and said, "Thank you, Captain, very much."

"Your new office will be ready for you to move into tomorrow," Chuck said as he added his congratulations. When Beth walked up to her desk back in the squad room, the phone was ringing. She answered it as she sat down.

"Ethan, it's good to hear from you; what's up?"

It had been about six months since Ethan had filed the DBA. He had decided early on to locate his office northwest of Syracuse so it would be easy for clients to find and yet be far enough away from the city so that it would not create a hectic off-hours lifestyle.

Ethan found an apartment he liked which was over an office, and using his negotiating skills, obtained both rent-free in exchange for remodeling them. The work was easy for Ethan since he had learned good carpentry skills from his dad.

It was cold in Syracuse, and had been snowing off and on for the past three days and on this day, Ethan sat in his high-backed chair, looking out the window from his room made warm and comfortable thanks to the combined heat from the gas fireplace and furnace He thought about how his business was making money so far handling mostly missing persons and insurance investigations; work that he thought was clean and satisfying compared to the police work in the vice squad he'd left. Although he was staring out the window, he didn't really see the beautiful snow-covered landscape. He was thinking about Beth, and how much he loved her.

Beth worked for the Baltimore police now, and at one time was a detective in Syracuse. It was six years ago since they'd broken off their relationship so Beth could take the job in Baltimore. He tried to talk her out of leaving without success. He'd only seen her for a period of about a week since that time. On a job he did for homicide, before leaving the SPD, he had followed a murder suspect to Baltimore and was able to get Beth assigned to work with him. The contact was just long enough to revitalize all his old feelings for her, and he hadn't been able to get her out of his mind since. The physical closeness of that assignment, and a small amount of socializing, resulted in his finding that she still had feelings for him, also. Since that last assignment, they had kept in close touch by phone, but he had not been able to talk her into moving back with him. He was now getting ready to call her and try again.

Forcing his thoughts back to the present, he looked at his watch and saw that it was almost 10 a.m., and he usually liked to be in the office by nine. When Ethan walked down the stairs from his apartment and into the fresh air, he felt warmth from the early morning sunshine, even though it was mid February.

He walked around the corner and stepped up the two steps to unlock his office door. The frosted glass had in large gold letters:

ETHAN WILLIAMS INVESTIGATIONS

Entering, he picked up his mail from the floor under the mail slot and headed for the oversized glass-topped oak desk that he had inherited from his father. Sitting down behind the desk he reached for the phone and dialed Beth's number.

"Hi, Beth."

"Ethan! What a surprise!"

There was a loud knock.

"Beth, hang on; there's someone at the door. Come in!" The door opened, and the man who stepped inside was short and weighed over two hundred pounds. His appearance, at first, made you think of a gorilla. "What can I do for you?" Ethan asked, as he stood, feeling irritated at having his call to Beth interrupted.

The visitor extended his hand and said, "I'm Harold Farnsworth and I'd like to hire you." Shaking the hand, Ethan said, "Have a seat, Mr. Farnsworth, and we'll talk about it." He turned his back to Farnsworth and said softly, "Beth, can I call you back in a little while? Someone just came into the office that I need to talk to."

"Sure," she said. "I plan to be here all morning."

Ethan hung up, sat down and said, "Okay, Mr. Farnsworth, it's your nickel!

CHAPTER TWO

Harold Farnsworth's appearance was neat, and his clothes well coordinated. His pants were black and went well with his blue and black plaid sport coat. He had chosen a blue shirt and a paisley tie to complete the outfit.

He said, "My father died of cancer last month, Mr. Williams, and named me executor of his will." Farnsworth fidgeted in his chair while his hands were clenched in his lap. "To carry out that duty, I need some help."

"Call me Ethan, and I'd like some background so I can understand your problem."

"Well, my father, Philip," Farnsworth continued, "started out in the concrete foundation business about fifty-five years ago, did very well, and continued to expand the business eventually building a factory. Within ten years, using the products from his factory, he began erecting multi-story buildings. That's when he started to get noticed, and soon after, was bought out by a conglomerate that hired him back to manage the construction end of the business. A few weeks before his death, he summoned me to his bedside. It was one of those out-of-town construction jobs that he wanted to talk to me about.

"My father was propped up in a hospital bed by pillows. The bed had been brought into the study of the house by Hospice when the doctor said he had less than a month to live. Hospice nurses made visits to the house as required to administer morphine for his pain. His skin was yellow and his mouth drawn. He patted his bed and said in a tired, raspy voice," 'Sit down here, Harold, close to me. I need to make a confession and ask for your help. I wanted to talk to you because I have faith in you, and I only have a short time to live.' He breathed heavily and coughed. 'I have re-written my will, and Charles here,' - he motioned to his attorney, Charles Boynton, sitting on the other side of the room – 'can tell you about that when we're done here.'

'In 1965 I did that office-building job in Baltimore. I don't want to make any excuses to you, so I'll make it short. Your mother's illness, combined with traveling a lot, resulted in my being very lonely. I had an affair with a woman named Rebecca Stone in Baltimore. I never stopped loving your mother, God rest her soul, and there was no real love between Rebecca and me. I'm sorry I didn't tell you earlier that somewhere out there, you, and your, brother and sister have a half sibling. I hadn't seen Rebecca for a couple of months and when I did, she told me she was pregnant. I offered her money for an abortion, but she wouldn't even consider it.'

She said, "You never told me you were married, and now you're just going to walk away. Well, the hell with you. I don't want your money. It's my baby and I'll have it, and love it, regardless of you." 'That was the last time I saw her. I'm very tired now, Son, and need to rest. Charles can fill you in on the rest.'

"After we left his room, Boynton explained that my father had made me Executor of his will. In addition to the normal executor duties, he assigned me the responsibility of finding our missing sibling. The terms of the Will are such that his estate, over twenty million, is to be divided equally amongst all the children including the illegitimate one. As an incentive to make sure the right thing is done, he has stipulated that no one inherits until the missing sibling is found. As a further incentive, besides picking me as his executor- because he trusts me - he has stipulated that I will inherit an extra million for finding our sibling."

"I said to Charles, "Boy, that's going to make Joyce and George happy."

He said, "There's not much they can do about it since it's spelled out in the will."

"My father fell into a comma and died two days after that meeting."

.

"Joyce and George are my brother and sister, Ethan. Neither one got along with our father. I don't get along too well with them myself. My brother is the oldest and has a college degree. Consequently, he thinks he's better and smarter than me. Maybe he is, but I didn't like being constantly reminded of it. Actually, he is a terrible businessman in spite of his CPA degree, and his accounting business is barely making it. I imagine they have been

13

waiting anxiously for this inheritance to infuse the business."

"My sister, on the other hand, was okay until she got married. After her marriage though, she changed. She hardly ever calls and we rarely get together any more. When we do, it's like she's putting on airs. Much like George, she thinks they're better then my wife, Becky, and me, but she doesn't actually say it, if you know what I mean. I think the change is due to the influence of her husband. She married a man, John Benton, who's plumbing and heating business is fairly successful."

"How about you, Harold, what do you do?" Ethan asked.

"I own a small book store in the mall," he said.

"That's about it, Ethan. The only lead I can give you concerning the whereabouts of this person is the mother's name, and where she lived at the time of the affair. I don't even have an address. I tried the white pages on the computer and had no luck."

"Okay, Harold, I think I can help you. My fee is four hundred a day plus expenses, and I require two days in advance. Either one of us can cancel the job at any time with two days notice." Harold swallowed hard as he listened to what it would cost. He thought for a moment and decided he would take the money from his savings and settle with the estate later.

As Farnsworth wrote the check, Ethan said, "I'll need the names, addresses and phone numbers of your brother, sister and your father's attorney. Also, I would like you to call the attorney and tell him I'll need a copy of the will."

Also, I would like you to call the attorney and tell him I'll need a copy of the will.

After Farnsworth left the office, Ethan picked up the phone and called Beth back. Beth jumped when the phone rang; bringing her out of the euphoria she was feeling from the early morning announcement of her promotion.

"Are you free to talk?" Ethan asked.

"Absolutely! Right now, I don't have a thing on my plate. I have my feet up, and am working on a cup of coffee."

"We haven't talked in almost a week and when I called a little while ago, I wanted to let you know I have been thinking about you, and still love you."

"That's nice." She smiled, thinking, even if he was just being nice, she liked it.

"Also, I wanted to ask you again if you would consider coming back to Syracuse."

"Ethan, we have this discussion every time we talk, which is at least once or twice a week, and you know how I feel. I love you as much as you love me, but why should I be the one to make all the sacrifices and move?"

"At least you have some friends here, Beth. I don't know anyone in Baltimore, and my business is here. There's nothing I want more then for us to get married and become partners. The business would then be called Williams Investigations."

"You've never mentioned marriage before. What's different?"

"I've given things a lot of thought since we worked together on that job a year ago. The intimate time we spent together then, and all the discussions we've had since, has made me realize that I can't function without you in my life. I know it's going to be a hard decision, but it makes a lot more sense to me for you to come back to Syracuse. What do you say?"

Beth took a big breath and exhaled noisily. "Your timing is lousy," she said.

"Why?" He asked.

"Oh, Ethan, I was promoted to lieutenant this morning. You know I love you, and if you had proposed yesterday, I would have accepted right off. Now, because of the promotion, I'm going to have to think about it."

"Beth," he said, "congratulations on your promotion! I think you really deserved it! I love you. Call me soon."

After Ethan hung up and was on his way to see Philip Farnsworth's lawyer, he thought, damn, I don't understand what her problem is. She should jump at the chance to come here and join the business. Well, I'm just going to keep badgering her until she gives in. And if she doesn't, then I'll go to Baltimore.

.

Charles Boynton was a thin, gray-haired man in his late sixties. He had had his own law practice since college, and had been Philip's attorney since he started the company. Now Charles was looking out the window of his third story office as he said, "Philip was a good man, Mr. Williams. He lived his life accordingly. The one exception was how he handled the affair, about which, I understand, Harold has told you.

During the last weeks of his life, he wrestled internally with himself, and externally to me as to how he could correct that mistake. As you know from talking with Harold, he was very serious in his goal."

16

Turning to his desk, Boynton picked up a yellow envelope and handed it to Ethan. "This is a copy of the Will that Harold instructed me to provide. Let me remind you that this document is to be handled as privileged information. If you are familiar with wills, you will find this one fairly standard except for the condition of finding the missing sibling. Do you have any questions, Mr. Williams?"

"Just one, Mr. Boynton, and then I'll get out of your hair. Is there a time limit on finding the sibling?"

"Philip decided he would leave that decision to Harold. If Harold decides at some point that the search is useless and has gone on long enough, then he has the power to end it. You see, Philip had complete faith in his son, Harold, to do what is right. Few parents have that kind of faith in a child." The lawyer added.

"I have to agree with that," Ethan said. "Thank you, Mr. Boynton, for your time."

CHAPTER THREE

Sara Stone was standing in the corporate boardroom with her own thoughts while she and the other vice presidents were awaiting the arrival of their boss, Jeff Johnson, the president and CEO of Teeter Tot Toys. Her peers were standing around joking, drinking coffee, and eating donuts. No wonder Herm Henderson's fat she thought. Although he didn't realize it, most of his clothes looked like shit on him. His shirts and coats looked like those on the guy in the old comic strip who had the chicken following him around to catch the buttons. Even Mark Hefron, whom she loved, was starting to get a little pot. Well, she wasn't going to eat donuts and get fat. Of course, her five foot five height helped her a little. Her thoughts wandered further, as they often did, to her background, and how she ended up where she was. She wondered if her father, whom she had never met, would have been proud of her accomplishments.

Perhaps her background helped her get where she was today more then she knew. Sara's mother, who had never married her father, Philip Farnsworth, and had never even told Sara his name, brought her up alone. Even Sara's grandmother didn't offer Rebecca Stone any help and because she loved her child very much and Sara had no father, Rebecca sacrificed much of her own life to give Sara as many advantages as possible. While working full time she assisted Sara in checking out various colleges to find one that would offer a scholarship.

Sara observed the struggles of her mother and vowed that she would have a better life. Knowing that there would be no better life without college, and no college without a scholarship, Sara maintained a three point five average in high school, which paid off in an academic scholarship to the University of Maryland. The scholarship, financial aid based on her mother's income and hard work on Sara's part, allowed her to graduate with a Bachelor's Degree in Mechanical Engineering.

Sara was very appreciative of her mother's efforts and sacrifices but hadn't shown it to her because of her refusal to tell Sara anything about her father. Now, Sara felt bad because her mother was in a nursing home with Alzheimer's and it was too late to let her mother know how she really felt.

After college, Sara went to work in the research department of Scientific Electronics Corporation in Baltimore, a supplier of aerospace hardware. While there, she took advantage of their Engineering Degree Program, earning a Masters and PhD in mechanical engineering.

After completing the engineering program, she proceeded to enroll in the Manufacturing Management Program. She would come out of this program as a first level Manufacturing Manager. She would then, have solid academic credentials and experience in Engineering, Manufacturing and Management, and could start looking for a better job.

After interviewing with a number of companies, she saw an ad in the paper one day for a manufacturing management position with Teeter Tot Toys, reporting to the president. Her first thoughts were whether she could handle a position reporting to the president and did she want to work for a commercial company? She would make her decision the next morning.

Over breakfast she made plans to try for an interview, which turned out to be tough! Jeff Johnson, the president for whom she would work, was a pleasant enough man, but asked some tough questions. In one case, she remembered, the question might have been downright embarrassing. He had said, "Sara, I can see that you have excellent academic credentials, but what have you done in manufacturing?"

Smiling, she remembered embellishing the little factory experience and the few management assignments she'd had during the training program at SEC. She had convinced him that it was adequate experience. She remembered another particularly hard question. Scratching his big nose, while smiling and staring at her with his dark eyes, he asked, "What's your philosophy on managing subordinates and interfacing their inputs with your peers and management?"

"I'm a manager's manager," she'd said. "I use each subordinate according to their strengths and, for the most part, trust his or her judgment and recommendations. Once I'm convinced on an issue, I'll run with it and fight for my position with no holds barred."

"What if you or your people are wrong?" he'd asked.

"Then, I'll go back, double check, and if I'm wrong, work my people's ass off and my own along with theirs to make it right." It was this last answer, Sara thought, that had significant influence in her getting the job after two more interviews. The meeting they were waiting for Johnson to convene was precisely about what you do when something goes wrong.

The boardroom door opened and closed, snapping Sara's thoughts back to the present. Jeff Johnson entered his hairdo blowing in his own breeze. "Good morning," he said, sitting down at the end of the table. Everyone else in the room found a seat.

CHAPTER FOUR

Jeff Johnson had been President and CEO of Teeter Tot Toys for five years, and the company's stock had doubled in value under his management. He was a hard-nosed, top-level manager who was critical and demanding of his people. Because he was like that, he often ignored his technical people's recommendations and decisions. He had no apparent sense of humor, dressed well, lived in a very large house in the best part of town, and drove the biggest Mercedes he could buy.

Jeff Johnson always sat at the end of the conference table with a window at his back and his secretary, Claire Roberts, at his side. The Vice Presidents of Operations, Finance, Human resources, and Engineering, along with other board members sat farther down the table. As he set his broad five-foot-eight inch body down, he took a quick look around the boardroom to make sure everyone was there, and said, "Let's get started."

After the minutes of the previous meeting had been read and approved, Johnson said, "All right, let's get on with the train problem."

Sara immediately stood. She had a slim build, a face with full lips, and a small nose that turned up slightly. The serious expression on her face made her look older than her thirty-five years. She had been V.P. of Operations at Teeter Tot Toys, for about three years now.

TTT was the toy division of Banner Enterprises and marketed, among many products, a five-car train set that had developed a problem with the adhesive holding it together. If a car was dropped, a small connector pin could break loose, and be a choking hazard to small children.

There had been a hundred thousand train sets sold and about a hundred cases of failure reported through their retailers, although there had probably been even more. Of the hundred, there was one known case of choking where the child did not suffer any real harm. The parents sued the company, and the case was settled out of court. They now had to decide if they should recall.

"Before we get into another big harangue," Sara said, "I want to restate my position, for the record, that the entire product should be recalled immediately."

"Sara, your position is noted, but it would be irresponsible not to consider all aspects of the issue before making that decision," Johnson said. "Now, I suggest you sit down and let me get on with the meeting."

Ever since the one time Sara had slept with Johnson and made it clear there would be no repeat episodes, his attitude toward her had changed, especially in situations like the current one, where others were present. It was like he was afraid someone would guess the truth if he acted otherwise. This time she thought stating her position on the recall up front would soften his attitude. Now, she felt it might have been a mistake, but at least it let her see his reaction, which obviously wasn't favorable.

That night, when she and Jeff had spent the night together was a perchance happening. They had been in a late out-of-town business meeting with a potential customer. Following the meeting, they took the president of the other company to dinner. During dinner, Sara drank a little too much wine. She hadn't been with the company very long, and was still somewhat overwhelmed by Jeff and her newfound way of life.

After dinner was over, and their guest had left the hotel, Jeff talked Sara into having a nightcap in his room to summarize the results of their meeting. Sitting close on the couch in his suite, Jeff turned and kissed her. Sara, finding it enjoyable in her inebriated state, responded favorably and Jeff took the lead from there. It wasn't long until they were in the bedroom.

The next morning when she woke up in his arms, she was astonished and ashamed. She remembered practically nothing about after dinner the night before. She knew Jeff was married, and being new with the company, she worried about how it would affect her job. She immediately decided to tell Jeff that it had been a mistake, apologize to him, and assure him it would never happen again. She slipped from his embrace and dressed as quickly as she could. He sat up in bed just as she was opening the door to leave.

"Where are you going?" he had asked.

"I'm going to my room and I'll see you at breakfast," Sara had answered.

Before Sara sat down, as she was asked to do, she said, "Jeff, There are still toys out there that represent a time bomb which could ruin our reputation AND the company. If news of the settlement gets out, as it probably will eventually, and there are other cases of choking that we settle in the meantime, it will be worse - not to mention the responsibility to the three and four year old kids who COULD get hurt by these toys."

"Nevertheless," the chairman said, I've asked Mark to give us an analysis of the financial impact of a recall and Herm to give us statistical analysis of the risk. Mark, I'd like you to go first."

Mark Hefron, Vice President of Finance, moved to the end of the table opposite Johnson and punched some keys on the laptop computer. His slide appeared on the projection display hanging from the ceiling. His jaw, which faced the audience, looked like it had been chiseled from some stone-like material. Being a personal friend of Sara's as well as a colleague, she knew he was not as fierce as he looked. He talked for about fifteen minutes on the costs associated with the advertising to make the recall happen, the cost of the product itself, and the cost of shipping. "As you can see," he said, pulling in his stomach and standing to his full six-foot height, the total cost would be approximately twelve million if everyone who bought a set responded, which they hardly ever do. This complicates matters because the trains still out there represent a potential future liability. From the financial standpoint, the twelve million eliminates the division's profit for the year and the stockholders would not be very happy. "With that said, I still think the prudent action, in the long run, is recall."

The chairman called on the Vice President of Quality Assurance, for his assessment.

Sara noticed that while Herm Henderson was bringing up his chart, his gray suit coat was open and the buttons on his shirt were strained against the belly hanging over his belt. In a nasal twang that filled the room, he said, "Let me pre-empt this pitch with a word of caution." Scratching his balding head through the thinning hair, he continued. "I'll be talking statistical projections, and there is no way of knowing for a fact if the numbers will or will not come to pass.

With approximately a hundred thousand train sets in the marketplace, a hundred reported failures, and one known accident there is at least one chance in ten thousand that more accidents will occur. That seems like a low risk, but let me remind you that the choking could result in brain damage or even death. We may have a liability out there in excess of a hundred million dollars. The risk is great enough to warrant recall."

"Sara, don't you have someone in your organization who interfaces with vendors?" Johnson asked,

"Yes, and he's in a negotiation meeting with SAA, as we speak. Of course, he won't talk about the lawsuit or the settlement. He will, however, stress the potential choking hazard. Because their product is defective, he'll push for them to cover the total cost of the product already built, and the cost of recalling the product in the field."

Sandy Boyle, V.P. of Engineering interrupted. "Come on, Sara. You don't really think they're going to go for that, do you?"

"No, normally, they'd take a position of only being responsible for the adhesive cost, but according to the report I got this morning, it looks like they'll give us something else; how much is yet to be determined." Sara smiled at him.

" I sure as hell hope so," Johnson said. "I suggest we proceed with the recall. If anyone disagrees, speak up now." Everyone was silent.

Although Boyle was quiet, his normally fair complexioned face was red. His people had specified the material and worked closely with Q.A. to make sure the vendors considered, understood the specifications, and had the capability to produce an acceptable product. Both his Engineering department, and Herm Henderson's Q.A. organization, felt heavy accountability associated with the problem.

"Fine," Johnson said. "Sara," he added, "Have a recall implementation plan on my desk by this time next week. If there's no other business, we're adjourned." Johnson left as quickly as he had arrived.

Sara went to the computer, opened an Office 2000 Word screen on the overhead monitor, pulled up a blank bullet chart and said, "Gentlemen, I suggest we stay right here and put together an outline for our plan. You heard Jeff. We have a week." A rumble of dissention arose, and several of the staff started to rise. "Hold it, guys," Sara called out, raising her voice, "I know he assigned me the responsibility, but we all have our share of this problem. It should be relatively easy, and a lot faster, if we get our hands around it while we're all here. If we don't, I'll be in each of your offices. If we have to do it one at a time, it's really going to be slow. I suggest we keep it simple. We'll list key milestones, responsibilities, and dates of completion." Using Office 2000 software, the formatting was done for them; all they had to do was fill in the blanks. It was a simple job; but not an easy one.

Sara worked most of the weekend and the following week on the plan. She interfaced in an expeditious manner individually with her peers scrubbed and rescrubbed the group developed plan until she felt it was ready. On Friday, she dropped the completed plan off with Jeff Johnson's secretary, left her Timonium office at 6:00 pm, and fought the heavy Beltway traffic on her way home to Towson.

She had just mixed herself a drink, and was about to sit down to watch the news on CNN when the phone rang.

"Sara, this is Jeff. I just looked at your plan. Are you guys trying to put the company out of business?"

Here it goes, she thought, rolling her eyes, as her stomach tightened. "What do you mean?"

Johnson, sitting at his desk while rubbing the back of his neck with his left hand, said, "I mean, in two months, we could have enough failures to break the company. The time has to be reduced."

"We worked like hell to get it down to two months. I don't see how it can be done any faster," she said.

"I won't accept anything more than a month, and preferably a hell of a lot less. Now, I expect to see another outline by noon on Tuesday showing how we're going to get there. Got it?"

"We'll try, but ..."

Johnson hung up before she could finish.

Sara took a sip of her martini and rested her head on the back of the couch, thinking about the problem. By the time she finished her drink she had an idea.

Mark Hefron also had been thinking about the timing issue and how the whole train problem would impact his year-end bonus. It was the annual bonus that had allowed him to buy the thirty-five foot Catalina sloop, "Sunset Pleasure." He and Sara had had some good times together, sailing on Chesapeake Bay. He had just finished showering and was putting on a white terrycloth robe when the phone rang. "Hello?"

"Mark, this is Sara. Do you have time to talk?"

"Sure. What's up?"

"I just got off the phone with Jeff. He rejected our plan based on the timing. We have to reduce the time to a month or less."

"Christ, I don't know how! Everyone thought we had wrung out everything we could."

"Mark, there is some time in there that is just plain waiting-for-things-to-happen time. We go to the distributors, who go to the retailers, who go to the customers, or we go to the TV stations and newspapers that go to the customers. Then, in all cases, we have to wait for

29

the customers to respond. I've got an idea, but don't know if it'll help.

These train sets sell for about fifty dollars. Most people probably charge them. Can the major credit card companies search their databases and send a notice directly to the customers who have purchased the trains? If so, I believe it can save a lot of time."

"Sara, what the hell have you been smoking? First, I think there'd be a privacy issue. Second, it would cost the companies money. Third, they're going to see no reason to help us, and I certainly wouldn't blame them."

"All right," Sara said, "So what do we do? Throw up our hands, give up, and then stand around until we're fired or the company goes under?"

Mark said, "I'll make some calls Monday, but don't get your hopes up."

"Mark, remember not to talk about the failures. Just say there's a possibility of a problem and we want to act fast before anything happens.

"Come on Sara; don't tell me how to do my job. I'll call you Monday around noon and let you know where we stand."

CHAPTER FIVE

Chris Blair was the first employee Sara had allowed her manager of manufacturing to hire. He was almost six feet tall and in his mid forties. His size helped in his position as manufacturing interface with vendors and subcontractors. Also, his broad nose with flared nostrils gave him a fierce look that served to intimidate the people with whom he had to negotiate with.

As Chris approached the adhesive vendor's plant, the sign at the entrance in large gold letters, SAA -- Sturgis Atkins Adhesives, caught his attention as it always did. They had been in business for about fifteen years, and Teeter Tot Toys was their biggest customer. In spite of the extra cautious business and technical approaches SAA practiced, problems did occasionally arise. The adhesive they sold under the name of Tough Bond, made up of epoxy and polyamide resins was such a problem. The meeting that Chris was headed into for talks between himself and SAA, personnel would address TTT's problem with Tough Bond failure.

In the small conference room at Sturgis Atkins Adhesives, Chris sat across the table from three of their personnel, and introductions were made across the table. SAA representatives were the Managers of Engineering, Quality Assurance and Manufacturing. After everyone shook hands and sat down, Chris said, "Guys, we have a serious problem. TTT has a significant amount of product in the field with defective SAA material in it. Let me hear some suggestions."

"We'll be glad to replace the material at no cost to Teeter," said Jocabowski, Manager of Manufacturing, frowning, while he scratched his vein-covered nose.

"Come on, Bruce, Chris said, your material is already in our product. What good's a replacement going to do?"

"We never warranty more than the material. Besides, it's your responsibility to test the material before you use it," Jocabowski shot back.

"So you're telling me that Teeter has to eat the cost of the labor spent putting your defective material into our product?"

"I guess so. At the most, we are responsible for replacement of the adhesive."

"Who, at SAA, allowed shipment of the adhesive?" Chris asked.

"I don't see the relevance of that," said Jester Galovatti, Manager of Engineering.

"The relevance," Chris said, "is that I'd like to hear something from that person."

"I guess I'm as responsible as anyone," said Barry Higgons, the Q.A. manager.

"Well, what do YOU say, Barry?"

"Normally we only take responsibility for the material and not the labor," Higgons replied.

"Well, let me tell YOU something;" Chris said, raising his voice. "This is NOT a normal situation. It's not only the adhesive. It's the costs associated with our material, labor, and shipment, the recalling of the product, receiving your new material, the re-building of our product, shipping of it, and God forbid, YOUR liability if one of the four-year old kids who use our product gets hurt or killed because of YOUR DEFECTIVE ADHESIVE! And I stress, YOUR liability, and, YOUR adhesive!" As he pointed his finger at Barry Higgons, he added, "That product out there a time bomb waiting to explode, and if it does, that liability is yours. The Sturgis managers looked at each other with sober expressions on their faces.

"But Chris..." Barry started to say.

"No buts Barry." Chris interrupted.

Now here's what I want. I want the material replaced at no cost to us. I want SAA to pay for the total cost to recall the TTT product containing the bad adhesive. That includes advertising, and shipping. Further, I want SAA to cover the cost of TTT labor to rebuild replacement product and the cost to reship it to the distributors and/or the customers."

"You can't expect SAA to give you a blank check," said Galovatti, "and besides, you guys have as much responsibility as we have.

Chris said "I'm asking you to pay for these specific things; TTT will cover the rest. The responsibility is not equal by any means, but we will estimate the costs and let you critique them so you can be satisfied that we're not being unreasonable. What I want right now is agreement, in principal, that you will cover these costs. Before you answer, let me re-emphasize the potential liability, if a child should choke to death because the defective adhesive fails on one of the items now in the field."

"Could you give us a moment alone?" Barry Higgons asked.

"Sure, I'll get a coffee in the cafeteria. Come get me when you're ready."

With Chris out of the room, Galovatti, smiling, was the first to speak. "Okay, Barry, since you say it's your fault, why don't you make a suggestion."

Higgons jumped to his feet. With sweat running down his face, he threw his pen on the table. "What the hell do you mean, MY fault? You may be joking, but this is no joking matter. Did you hear what he said?" They plan to put all the blame on us if there is a field catastrophe. I didn't specify the goddamn resins!"

"No, but you sure as hell let it get into the product."

"All right," said Jocabowski, his blond hair hanging down over his sweaty forehead. "We're not going to solve the problem by accusing and blaming each other. I think Chris is asking for the moon to see how much he can get. We're going to have to give something. I suggest, in addition to replacement material, we offer to pay for the labor to rebuild what they have in the field. It'll cost us, but it's a hell of a lot less then he's asking for, and considering the possible liability, it's not such a bad deal.

We may have to give even more, but we can't make these kinds of decisions here. We'll have to take it up the line."

"Okay, I'll go get him," Galovatti said, "and we'll tell him we need more time."

Back in the conference room, Jocabowski told Chris they needed time to discuss things with their management. Chris said, "Okay, but don't take too long." He turned and left quickly without saying anything further. Let them sweat over what I asked for, he thought. If I don't hear from them tomorrow or the next day, I'll give them a call.

CHAPTER SIX

While Sara was in the boardroom at TTT, and Chris was negotiating with SAA, Ethan was in Syracuse working on a job he had going before the Farnsworth case.

An individual named Waterhouse had filed a disability claim against Equity Insurance. The insurance company's doctor couldn't find a reason for the pain in Waterhouse's back, and suspected he was trying to cheat the company. The Claims Manager called Ethan to check into the validity of the claim.

Ethan sat in his car down the street from the apartment. This had been his practice since he started the case. He would sometimes use his own car, sometimes a borrowed car, and sometimes a rental. This, in conjunction with parking in different locations for different times, wearing different hats and some times false mustaches and/or beards, kept him from being noticed.

On this particular day when he was bored with the waiting, he let his mind drift to thinking what it would be like to be married to Beth. She could get her PI license and become his partner, as well as his lover and wife. Not lover in the modern sense of a live-in sex partner, but a life-long partner with a romantic commitment of true love and devotion between the two of them. They would be able to spend time working together, sharing their feelings about the job and having a great time at home after a hard day's work.

It was about ten-thirty when he saw Waterhouse's car approaching the apartment house. Ethan set the paper aside and put his coffee in the cup holder as the suspect pulled up in front of the building. Ethan took a picture of him as he got out, went around the car and opened the trunk. He took a large box, almost two feet square, out of it and started for the stairs leading to the apartment. Ethan read the writing on the box through the camera's telephoto lens, 25 INCH RCA TELEVISION. It was obviously a heavy box, and not one that could be carried up a set of stairs by a person with a bad back. It would appear that Ethan had hit pay dirt this time. He continued photographing Waterhouse until he was near the top of the stairs; then he headed for Equity Insurance.

He made some notes and left the stakeout. This cleaned up all his old business and now he could concentrate on the Farnsworth case. He went to see Harold's brother-in-law.

* * *

Benton's business was located in a small shopping plaza in Liverpool and had separate doors marked 'Plumbing' and 'Heating'. Ethan entered the plumbing side. He walked past the displays and approached a girl at a desk just inside the railing separating the display floor from the office area. She was filing her nails and chewing gum. "Is John Benton around?" he asked.

"He's in his office back there," she said, snapping her gum and pointing to the rear of the store with her nail file.

"I'd like to see him."

"Do you have an appointment?" she asked in a high-pitched nasal voice.

"No."

"Who should I say wants to see him and what about?"

"Just give him this," Ethan said, clenching his jaw and throwing his card on her desk.

She was back in a few minutes and said, "You can go in."

John Benton was in his mid thirties, under six feet tall and going bald. It was obvious that he worked out.

"What can I do for you, Mr. Williams?" he asked as Ethan entered.

"I'll be quick. I just wanted to meet you and ask if you have any information that might help me find your missing sibling."

"I'm sure Harold told you that Joyce and her father weren't very close, and therefore, I was even less close."

"He did tell me that, but I thought you might have overheard something even though you weren't close. You know, sometimes you overhear something or get an inference that might help."

38

"I'm afraid I can't think of anything. The old man was always civil to me, but I can't recall ever having a serious conversation with him, let alone something as intimate as an affair. Sorry."

"Well, thanks, John, for your time, but you know, you've got a lot at stake in this inheritance. If you know any of his friends well enough, you might explore the subject with them. Here's my card, if you should come up with something."

Ethan's next stop was Harold's sister's house. It was a small two story colonial: one railing on the porch was loose and sagging, several pieces of siding were missing above the porch roof, paint was peeling from the window frame on the porch and the window glass was cracked. Ethan parked on the driveway behind a large camper.

A plump woman in her mid thirties wearing a green sweat suit answered the door. Her hair was tied in a ponytail, she was breathing hard and sweating. "Can I help you?" she asked.

"Joyce Benton?"

"Yes."

"I'm Ethan Williams," he said, pulling out his wallet to show her his PI license, "and, as you probably know, Harold hired me to find your missing sibling. I apologize for not calling ahead, but I would like to talk with you for a few minutes."

"Okay, come on in. Don't mind how I look," she said, still out of breath. Ethan wondered if she had been thin once and was now battling hard to regain the figure she had lost.

"What can I do for you?" she asked, starting to get her wind back.

"I'm looking for leads that might give some direction to my search. Right now, all I know is the mother's name and that she used to live in Baltimore. I thought you might have heard something more from your father over the years that might help."

"I'm sorry, Mr. Williams; I can't add anything to what you just stated. Now, I really do need to get back to my exercising."

"Thanks for your time, Joyce. It'll be to everyone's advantage if we can come up with some kind of lead." Frustrated, he gave her his card, and said, "Give it some serious thought and call me if you come up with anything."

CHAPTER SEVEN

Beth was doing paperwork when the phone rang. "Hi, Ethan, I thought I was supposed to call you when I'd made a decision."

"You were, and I'm not calling to pressure you. The reason I called has to do with a case I'm working on. I'm looking for the daughter of a woman who lived in Baltimore in 1965. Could you do a DMV check and see if there is an address for her?"

"Did you check the phone book?"

"Yeah, and the Internet. Also, I could have done the DMV check from here, but I decided I'd rather talk to you than to a computer." He smiled.

"Well, it's easier to ask than to look, and I figured that's what you did." she said jokingly.

"You want to check on the mother or the daughter?"

"The mother, Ethan answered, "I don't know the daughter's name."

"You know, Ethan, this is against the rules."

"I know. Her name is Rebecca Stone."

"You're lucky I'm a lieutenant now." She entered the name into her computer. "Got a pencil and paper handy?"

"Yeah."

"It's 2546 Eastern Avenue. "Ethan, I know you don't want to pressure me, but you could at least ask me if I've been thinking about an answer to your proposal."

"I'm sorry, Sweetheart, I didn't mean to seem disinterested, but I really didn't want to put pressure on you. Have you been thinking about it?"

"I've made my decision, Ethan." She paused and smiled. The pause made Ethan hold his breath until she said, "And the answer is yes. Also, I've decided I'll move to Syracuse. I…"

"That's wonderful Beth!" he said, raising his voice an octave and interrupting her.

"Isn't it though?" she said, still smiling. "Now,   I started to say why I was putting off telling you. This week, two undercover detectives from another division were assigned to me. Their drug case is about to come down with a lot of arrests. Since I just made lieutenant, I want the arrests to my credit before I leave the force."

"I can understand that, Beth."

"When will you be coming to Baltimore?" she asked.

"I'll come down this weekend, and we'll celebrate."

"Sounds great." There was a knock at the door. "I have to go Ethan, someone's at the door. Call me soon, Love, bye."

After hanging up the phone, she yelled, "Come on in." Two men came through the door. The first had about a week's growth of beard and was dressed in jeans, Colts sweatshirt and dirty sneakers. He said, "Good morning' Lieutenant." He plopped into one of the padded armchairs in front of her desk.

The other man was black, sported dreadlocks and was dressed in a manner similar to the first. "Top of the morning, Lieutenant." He took the other chair in front of her desk, leaned back and draped his leg over one of the arms.

"Good morning, Frank, Jason," she said, nodding to each of them. "What's the latest?"

"The big buy's on Friday as planned," Jason said. "The amount's fifty thou. They think we'll make the exchange, and head straight for Rochester."

Frank added, "As we said the other day, we expect the big cheese to be there on Friday."

"Have you set the time and place?" Beth asked.

"Yeah." The rear of the side parking lot of Burdines on Broadway at seven p.m."

"I want to be in on the bust," and I want you to make sure there is plenty of coverage to prevent any foul ups. Got it?"

"Right." They chimed together.

"Okay, That's it for now. Let's get together Friday morning to go over the details on timing and backup support. Also, if it looks like it's not coming down Friday night, let me know."

Beth was standing in her office when she looked at her watch. I wish they'd get here, she thought. She was waiting for Jason and Frank to arrive for their Friday morning meeting. They needed to discuss the details of the arrest tonight. Exchange in an open parking lot would probably be trouble. Beth didn't care what they said. She would feel better if the drug dealers were confined inside a building where they could be surrounded and the entrances controlled. She liked the idea of having her old boss, Chuck Jones, and his detectives for backup.

Jason and Frank arrived at her office. Even though they weren't late, she said, "It's about time." Chuck and his two detectives followed them shortly Beth stated her concern about the exchange taking place in an open parking lot.

"As I understand it," Chuck contributed, "my guys will be behind the building in their car, and we'll all be listening in on the wires being worn by your guys. Their position back there will block escape around that side which is dark and isolated. Because of that isolation, I suggest you and I back them up."

"As soon as we make the deal for the dope," Frank said, "we'll announce it so everyone can hear. We'll have squad cars on Broadway, two to the north, and two to the south, ready to come in immediately. They'll be listening in on the wire too, so they can make their move at the right time."

"I don't see how anything could possibly go wrong," Jason, said.

There are a million things that could go wrong, Beth thought. She said, "There's no way of knowing what these crazy druggies might do. What happens if they check and find the wires?"

"Then we'll yell, 'HEY!' Chuck chimed in, "and that will be the signal for everyone to come in, surround them and make the arrests."

"All right," Beth said, "I guess we're as ready as we'll ever be. Chuck, you drive, since your car is black and will be less conspicuous. Okay, I guess that's it. Chuck, pick me up here in the parking lot at six, and if everything goes as planned, we'll see you guys after it goes down."

Ethan had called Beth earlier in the week and told her he was going to drive down Friday morning so they would have the whole weekend to celebrate. He was now wondering if that had been a good idea. The weatherman on the eleven o'clock news had just predicted lake effect snow for early in the morning. After giving it some thought, he decided to stay with the original plan, except he would leave at ten o'clock instead of seven, so the Highway Department would have time to plow and salt the roads.

Ethan was making pretty good time. He had been right about the plows. The roads were fairly clear. They had been plowed and sanded. In Pennsylvania, the roads were covered with considerable snow. About half way between Binghamton and Scranton, he decided to stop for lunch, and a badly needed break. As he put on his blinker for the approaching exit from Interstate 81, he looked to his left and thought he was being crowded by the tractor-trailer that was passing him. It was hard to tell for sure, because the visibility was so bad.

He looked back and forth between the semi and the approaching exit. The semi was almost past him. It was throwing sand, snow and water on his windshield. The windshield wipers and washers couldn't remove it fast enough for him to see very well. The tractor was even with his front bumper. The exit-ramp was about a quarter mile ahead. The driver of the tractor-trailer hit his breaks and the rig jackknifed. The right end of the trailer's bumper caught and locked with Ethan's left front fender. His mind panicked. He said, "Oh shit, that stupid bastard! They're supposed to know how to drive!" Sweat formed on his forehead. He tried to jerk to the right and use the off ramp to escape, but couldn't pull free. He wondered if he should speed up while trying to get free. No, that would probably take him towards the truck, and might throw him under the wheels because of the direction in which the trailer was sliding.

His heart was racing as he was being dragged along by the semi. The end of the guardrail that separated Interstate 81 from the exit ramp, rapidly approached. The semi's position worsened, turning his car to a more precarious angle. Ethan was still trying to assess his imminent danger, and quickly realized that the semi would be between him and the guardrail, but it was very likely that the semi would flip over, and if it did, it would take him with it. He heard the tractor crash into the guardrail and was absolutely helpless to do anything to stop what he knew was going to happen.

CHAPTER EIGHT

He felt the car leave the road. It leaned to one side and tipped up on its end. He saw the side of the trailer, the lettering barely visible through the mud and snow. Then he was falling. The car landed upside down with a loud crushing sound. He saw stars, and then everything went black.

The world was upside down and white with an eerie red glow. He could hear voices, but couldn't see who was talking. It all came back to him now. He had been in a car crash with a semi. He was still strapped in the upside down car. The pain in his back was so bad he could hardly stand it, and he couldn't move. Then the car door was opened and he saw a face looking at him.

"Sir, can you hear me? How do you feel?"

Ethan spoke in a pain-racked raspy voice. "M…my… back… h…hurts…li…like hell, and I… can't m…move."

"Lie still," the man said, as he gave him a shot.

Ethan relaxed, and soon was dreaming about Beth.

"Beth, that you?" he called out.

"Mr. Williams, can you hear me?" a voice asked.

"Beth?" she answered.

"Nurse, has he said anything," the doctor asked, as he entered Ethan's room. "He's semi-conscious and has been asking for someone named Beth"

"I just looked at the X-rays. He has a broken back. Fortunately, the vertebrae have not been crushed. It's just a compression fracture. I'll get to work making a mold to fit him with a brace. Do we have a number for someone we can call?" the doctor asked.

"I found a phone number in his wallet for an Elizabeth Jordon. Must be the Beth he's been asking for. She lives in Baltimore." The nurse said.

"If you can give her a call, Nurse, I'll talk to her." The nurse dialed the number and handed the phone to Dr. Cook. "Ms. Jordon, this is Dr. Cook at Mercy Hospital in Scranton Pennsylvania. Do you know a Mr. Ethan Williams?"

"Yes, he's my fiancé," Beth said, "What's happened?" Her expression turned serious, and her hand started to shake.

"He's going to be okay, but there's been an automobile accident, and I'm afraid your fiancé has a fractured back."

"Oh my God!"

"As I said, he'll recover, but it'll take a while for complete healing. We can fit him with a brace and have him up and around in two to three weeks. From that point on, he'll be able to do as much as he feels like while the healing continues," the doctor explained.

Beth wiped tears from her eyes and asked, "May I come see him?"

"Yes, but there's no rush because he's medicated for the pain, and is sleeping most of the time. We'll fit him for the brace tonight, and late tomorrow or Sunday morning, he should be fairly alert."

"Okay, I'll plan to be there by noon tomorrow. And Doctor, this is my cell phone. If anything should go wrong, you call me immediately, okay?"

"I'll do that, Ms. Jordon, and I'll see you tomorrow. I'll put my nurse on, and she can tell you how to get here."

It was Friday, and the drug arrests were planned for that night. Beth would head for Scranton as soon as it was over.

"I tell you, Cortez, don't sweat it."

Cortez was looking out the tenth floor window of the hotel room with his back to his two subordinate's wondering why the hell he had ever gotten into a business which caused him to deal with assholes like these two. He could hardly stand them, and wasn't even sure he could completely trust them either. Down deep, though, he knew he would tolerate anything for the money.

He said, "You'd better be goddamn right this time, is all I can say."

"Look, Cortez, we've worked these two for over a year," one of the guys said in a low pitch voice with a Brooklyn accent, "selling them small quantities. We've increased the amount every few months and there's never been a problem. They've always been on time at the places we pick and always had the money. We've taken extra precaution this time because you'll be with us. Before, we always met inside, but this time the meet'll be out in the open so we'll have lot'sa room to maneuver in case somethin' goes wrong. Also, you can stay by the car until we check them out and check the money. Then you can bring the merchandise up."

"Okay," Cortez said, "now get out of here so I can rest. Pick me up at six."

Cortez was waiting in the lobby when his men arrived. They didn't waste any time or exchange any words. Cortez rose and headed for the door with his underlings falling in behind. Outside, one of the men left the group and headed for the parking lot. Cortez and the others followed him to the waiting car.

In the side parking lot of Burdines, Beth, Chuck, and their detectives had been in position since five forty-five. When Jason and Frank saw a car come around the corner from the front of the store, turn off its lights and turn them back on, they got out of the car. The other car's lights went off again, and the three drug dealers got out. Frank and Jason moved forward and placed a briefcase on the hood. There was enough light in the parking lot to just make them visible. Two of the men approached. One said, "Let's see in the case." Frank opened it and tipped it up slightly. One of the men looked in and said, "Okay, close it." Then he turned and waved to Cortez standing by the car and said, "You," pointing to Jason, "Come over here."

Jason walked over cautiously and said, "What?" He quickly grabbed Jason's shirt with both hands and ripped it open. "HEY!" Jason yelled.

The man with the Brooklyn accent cried, "WIRE!" As he pushed Jason against Frank. Both dealers ran towards Cortez and the car. The man who had pushed Jason grabbed the briefcase of money from the hood of the car as he passed.

Over the radio, Beth yelled," Move in! They've been made!" Beth, Chuck, with his two detectives, and the squad cars all converged on the three drug dealers. As they stopped their cars and got out, the three men began shooting. Chuck's detectives were the first to return fire followed closely by Beth and Chuck. The uniformed officers were the last to contribute to the return of fire. About twelve shots were fired without noticeable result. Seeing an opportunity, Beth stepped from behind the car door that she was using for a shield, and fired a shot. It hit the man who had been waiting by the other car. Before she could pull back to cover behind the door, she screamed and fell backwards.

"Beth," Chuck yelled, as he scrambled around the car, "are you okay?" There was no answer.

After Beth had shot the man by the car and one of the other men had gotten off the shot that hit her, Frank fired a shot that hit the third man. With two of the drug dealers down, the third raised his hands and yelled, "Don't shoot, I give up." The uniformed officers rushed forward, and cuffed the three while Frank and Jason joined Chuck to see if they could help with Beth. "There's nothing you can do, fellows," Chuck said, "I've already called an ambulance. One of you can call an ambulance for those two, pointing to

51

the two who were wounded, and make sure all three have their rights read to them."

Johns Hopkins Hospital Emergency Room was like any other metropolitan hospital ER. Busy. The paramedics had responded quickly to Chuck Jones's call for help. The ambulance was met at the Emergency Room door, and Beth was rushed straight to an examining room. The Medics had telephoned ahead on the way in and asked that a surgeon be standing by when they arrived.

The doctor examined Beth's head wound and determined that she had suffered a severe concussion and was in a coma. Fortunately, the bullet had hit a glancing blow so had not penetrated the skull.

"She might come out of the coma right away, or she might never come out," Dr. Cook had said before admitting Beth, and sending her to intensive care. He then went to the waiting room to give Chuck the bad news.

Beth had told Chuck about Ethan's accident and that she planned to visit him on Saturday at Marcy Hospital in Scranton. He went to a pay phone, called the Hospital, and asked to speak to Ethan. "Ethan, this is Chuck Jones. How are you feeling?"

"I'm feeling pretty good. They have me in a brace and are giving me pain pills. I'm surprised to hear from you, what's up?"

"Ethan, I've got some really bad news. Beth was shot tonight in the line of duty."

"Oh, my God! Where? How bad?"

"She's not dead, but she was shot in the head."   Then Chuck told him what the doctor had said.

"How's she doing?"

"She's in a coma, and the doctor says all we can do is wait."

With tears in his eyes, Ethan sniffled. "We plan to get married. She has to make it! As soon as I can get out of here and can drive, I'll rent a car and come straight down. If she wakes up before I get there, tell her I sent my love and am on my way."

CHAPTER NINE

Sara was sitting in her office at TTT preparing a memo to Jeff Johnson. The telephone rang. She saved her work on the computer and picked up the phone. "Hello."

"Hi, Sara, this is Mark."

"Mark! How'd you make out?" Sara laid her pen on the desk and pushed her computer keyboard out of the way.

"I contacted most of the big credit card companies. They listened when I asked them about sorting their customer database and sending out recall notices.

"Good, Mark, what did they say?

"They responded as I expected. There was interest in preventing a problem, but they won't assume any expense.

Didn't you tell them we'd pay?" Sara asked.

"Yeah, and I asked them to price the job. That's when they let the other shoe fall. Everyone I talked to, with slight variations, said, 'In this day of prolific lawsuits, we're afraid of the violation of privacy. Sorry, we can't help.' It looks like we're back where we started."

"That's just great, Mark, what do you suggest we do now?"

"I'm sorry, Sara, I know you're stuck with trying to reduce the time on the recall, and I wish I could help, but I have no idea. I suggest getting the staff back together to see if the group can come up with something else."

"Shit," she said, "It's ironical. Chris Blair called this morning. He's gotten the adhesive vender to agree to pay for the entire recalled product and, in addition to the replacement of the adhesive. They figured absorbing that cost would be a cheap way to get us to share the liability. That savings won't mean a hell of a lot if we can't get the product back in time to prevent a serious accident. I'll revise the plan this afternoon, and shorten the time by a month. We'll all get together this afternoon and figure out something to support the change. No matter what, I have to go back to Johnson tomorrow. Thanks, Mark, for your support and fast response on this thing. It sucks that it didn't work out. I'll see you later." She hung up.

After a week in the hospital, Ethan felt good. The brace, along with an occasional pill, allowed him to walk with very little discomfort. He would be discharged tomorrow and could get back to his life. There wasn't much damage to his backbone, and he was healing quickly. He didn't look forward to wearing the brace for another two to four weeks, but the doctor didn't give him any choice. He arranged for a rental car to be delivered to the hospital when he was released, and he'd been calling Johns Hopkins every day to check on Beth. There had been no change, but he was still very anxious to see her.

The insurance companies agreed the accident was the other guy's fault. His car had been declared a total loss and was hauled in by the police who recovered his suitcase, and had it delivered to him. The insurance company was sending him a check for the car

Ethan was driving the rental car south on Interstate 81 and thinking about his life before the accidents. He and Beth were about to get married six years earlier when Beth was on the force in Syracuse. She was still a plainclothes cop, and he had just gotten his detective's badge. They'd been living together for about three years. Just as Ethan was about to propose, she was offered the detective's job in Baltimore.

"You can't expect me to quit my job and move," Ethan had said to her at that time.

She countered, "You expect me to pass up an offer that I've been working towards for five years?"

"Yeah, but at least you've got a job here."

After considerable arguing, Beth said, "I'll tell you what, Ethan. You keep your damn job, and I'll move and take the job I've always wanted."

That was it until about a year ago when Ethan was given that special assignment to support the homicide division on a murder case that took him to Baltimore where he and Beth worked with each other, and dated during off-duty hours. That time together rekindled all the old fires they thought had been extinguished when Beth moved to Baltimore. Over the course of the year since then, their relationship blossomed; he had proposed, Beth had accepted, and then the accidents.

Ethan passed Harrisburg, took Interstate 83 into Baltimore, and went straight to the hospital. He opened the main door went to the information desk and asked the attendant what room Beth Jordon was in. The aid checked her list and said, "She's in intensive care and may have no visitors except family."

Lying, Ethan said, "I'm her brother. Can you tell me how to get there?"

"Take the elevator to the third floor. The nurse's station there can direct you."

On the way to the elevator, Ethan concentrated on the black and white tile on the floor trying not to think about what he was going to see. It seemed to take the elevator forever to arrive. Finally, he reached the nurse's station.

The nurse said, "When you called this morning, I told you our visiting hours are 9:00 to 11:00 am and 2:00 to 4:00 pm. But, since you've come so far today and it's almost 4:00, I'm going to let you stay until five.

"Thanks," he said.

Ethan had been calling the hospital every day, and thought he was prepared to accept what he would see. He wasn't. As he entered Beth's room, a lump immediately formed in his throat. She was lying on her back, eyes closed, and tubes running from her nose, mouth and arm. She looked dead. Ethan started to cry. He sat next to her bed and took her hand. Sobbing, he said, "Oh, Beth, I love you so! What will I do if you don't make it?"

He thought about the wonderful times they'd had together in Syracuse. They'd played tennis, ice-skated, golfed and gone to ball games. They'd taken sailboat rides out of Oswego harbor, gone to movies, and had dinner at all the good restaurants. Would they be able to do any of those things again? He put his head in the crook of his elbow on the bed and continued to cry. After a while, he pulled out his handkerchief and wiped his eyes before leaving her side.

He blew his nose and recovered his composure in the waiting room by himself. He could smell the coffee across the room, but he had no stomach for anything to eat or drink after what he had just experienced.

The doctor arrived. He was young and, to Ethan, looked like a teenager.

"I'm Dr. Lee, Mr. Williams, and am very sorry about Ms. Jordon. I'm afraid the prognosis is not very good. I must tell you that the longer she remains in the coma, the less likely she is to recover."

"Is there anything I can do to help her chances, Doctor?"

"There is a theory that if one in a coma is talked to often, it may speed up his or her recovery. Some loved ones have practiced this and believed it helped. It is not up to me to judge such a subjective theory. I can only say there is no scientific evidence to support it. We will watch her very closely and make sure she gets the very best care. Good luck, Mr. Williams, and if you have any questions, the nurses can always reach me." He shook hands with Ethan, turned, and left the room.

Boy, he's a cold son-of-a-bitch, Ethan thought, as he started back to Beth's room. Once there, he leaned over, and kissed her lightly on the lips. He felt the chill of the oxygen tube extending from her nose and the feeding tube from the corner of her mouth. It brought tears to his eyes again. He said, "Beth, I love you and I know you have the strength to pull through this. I have your ring waiting. We'll be married as soon as you're well enough and ready. Goodbye, Darling, I have to go now, but I'll see you tomorrow."

He went to the motel and checked in. After he took a shower, he called Chuck Jones at police headquarters. "Hi, Chuck, it's Ethan."

"Hi, Ethan, how's Beth today?"

"No better and the doctor says the prognosis is not good. Did you get the Bastards that did this to her?"

"Yeah, one's in jail, and the other two are in the hospital. We got'em dead to rights on drug charges and attempted murder. There are plenty of witnesses to the attempted exchange of drugs for money. Are you staying in Baltimore for awhile, Ethan?"

"Yes, at least until Beth's okay. I'll check on her every day and when I can't do anything else, I'll work on the Farnsworth case. I think I told you it's tied to Baltimore.

"Yeah, you did. Remember, if there's anything I can do to help you or Beth, let me know."

"Thanks."

CHAPTER TEN

It was early afternoon and Sara was at the conference table in her office talking with the other vice presidents. "This is stupid," Sandy Boyle said. "We can go to the distributors, the retailers, the customers, and the media at the same time or through the normal serial chain. Either way, the total recall time comes out the same."

"I agree," Sara said. "We'll let the plan stand as it is. I'll see Johnson this afternoon." The meeting ended and everyone left.

Sara grimaced, and leaned back in her chair. "Damn Jeff Johnson." It always made her mad when she had to try and save his ass after he'd done something as stupid, as he did in the case of testing the adhesive for the train sets. If he'd listened to Quality, instead of trying to save a buck, this mess would never have happened.

The telephone rang, bringing Sara out of her deep thought.

"Hello." She twisted her head in a circular pattern to relieve the stiffness in her neck from stress.

"Ms. Stone, This is the Deaton Nursing Home. I have some bad news for you. Your mother managed to get free of her restraints this morning and fell out of bed. I'm afraid she has broken her hip. We sent her to Mercy Hospital about fifteen minutes ago."

Sara's face got red. Venting her stress and frustration from work as well as her anger at the nursing home, she said, "How the hell can you goddamn people be so irresponsible? She's in that home to be taken care of, not to be tied down and forgotten. Tell me why you and that shithole you work at shouldn't be sued." Without waiting for an answer, she continued, "Next, I suppose you're going to tell me that there won't be a room for my mother when she gets well enough to come back."

"Oh, no, Ms. Stone. We guarantee that there'll be a place for her when she's ready to return. You must understand that Mrs. Stone is getting the best of care. The nurse turned her back for just a few minutes when the accident occurred. It's very unfortunate and we are very sorry."

"As you should be!" Sara said, gritting her teeth and hanging up. She hadn't been to see her mother in a long time. Nevertheless, she couldn't forget when she put her mother in there. The Home wasn't any worse, or any better than the others. They all had some degree of bad odor and help that was rude, mean, uncaring, or just plain incompetent. In addition, such places were all over-priced.

*   *   *

The woman at the reception desk directed Sara to her mother's room where she found her lying on her back with a huge cast on her left hip, which extended down onto her thigh. She was asleep. Sara looked at her mother with sympathy. She regretted now that she had not been a more agreeable and appreciative daughter. Her bad attitude had been because her mother was unmarried and not willing to say anything about her father.

Now that Sara was a success and could pay her mother back for all the help she had been, it was too late. She was senile. As bad as things had been between them in the past, she loved her now, and wondered if she had always loved her and didn't realize it, or if she had just come to love her since she no longer could care for herself.

As Sara stood in the doorway thinking back, tears welled up as her mother moved. She went in and took her frail hand. "Hello, Mother." Rebecca Stone looked at her through glassy eyes and gave a weak smile. "Are they taking good care of you, Mother?" There was no response. Sara just stood there holding her hand.

The nurse came in and proceeded to check Rebecca's vitals.

"Nurse, has she spoken since she was brought in?" Sara asked.

"No. She was taken straight to an operating room to work on her hip, and sedated. She's been on sedatives since the operation to minimize her pain."

"Is the doctor still in the hospital?" Sara asked.

"I think so. Would you like me to page him?"

"Yes."

The doctor entered the room and asked, "Are you Rebecca's daughter?"

"Yes. How's she doing, Doctor?"

"Pretty well, considering her age. It was a clean break and we were able to get by with one pin. She should be lucid by this time tomorrow, and able to return to the Home next week. With therapy, she might be able to get around with a walker in a month or two."

After the doctor left, Sara noticed her mother was asleep again. She looked at her watch. It was three o'clock. She had to go back to meet with Johnson, as much as she dreaded it. She would come back to the hospital after the meeting, and maybe her mother would be awake then.

CHAPTER ELEVEN

Because his search for Sara was at a standstill, Ethan would call Harold and give him a report.

"It's been almost a month, Ethan!"

"Harold, what can I say? I'm standing here in a brace with a broken back, and my fiancée is in the hospital in a coma."

"My brother and sister want results," his client said.

"I'm in Baltimore, and I'll work on your case as soon as things are back to some semblance of order."

"When'll that be?"

"It'll be when it it'll be. If that's not satisfactory, you can find someone else."

"I don't want someone else; I need results!"

"Good, Harold, You can count on me getting on with your case as soon as possible, and I won't bill you for anything until I do."

He said, "Okay, Ethan, and hung up.

It was one o'clock in the afternoon before Ethan was able to get to the hospital.

He had expected a little more understanding and sympathy from Farnsworth. Out of character, Ethan had gotten very angry while talking to him. The reason being, that he was feeling sorry for himself and Beth. Harold was apparently taking a lot of heat from his brother and sister to clear up the case so they could get their money. Ethan decided that after he visited Beth, he would call him and have a more civilized conversation.

The hospital was as depressing as usual. Patients were limping along the hall or being pushed in wheel chairs. Some hobbled on crutches, some shuffled along in robes with their heads down, and others were led through the halls. And that was before getting to the Intensive Care Unit. Of course, thought Ethan, given a choice, it's much better to be able to move, even if it's on a gurney.

As he approached Beth's room, he saw that the drape was pulled across where the open door was. As he approached it, a nurse with white hair and glasses who almost ran into him opened the drapery. "Oh, I'm sorry," she said, stepping around Ethan as the drape swooshed close behind her.

Ethan asked, "Is something wrong?"

"Oh, no," she said. "I just gave her a bath, checked her tubes and turned her slightly. We move her around periodically to prevent skin irritation."

"Has there been any change in her condition, Nurse?"

"I only work afternoons, but there's nothing marked on her chart. I'm sorry."

"That's okay. Do you know when the doctor will be in?"

"He usually makes his rounds about three o'clock unless he has an emergency." As she turned to leave, she said, "If you need anything, I'll be at the station over there. If the doctor comes in, I'll tell him you're here."

Ethan sat at the edge of the bed. "Beth, I hope you can hear me. I want you to know I love you with all my heart and am very sad to see you just lying here and not able to respond. I lie awake at night praying for the time when we can make love again, get married, and get on with the rest of our lives. I pray you can hear me, and find some comfort and peace of mind from my being here." Ethan gripped her hand, leaned over, and kissed her on the cheek. Then he left the room. He told the nurse he'd be in the waiting room and would like to see the doctor when he came in.

He was looking through a newspaper when Dr. Lee walked in, dressed in a light tan sport coat. He looked like a different person out of the white hospital coat and in street clothes.

"Hello, Mr. Williams, I just came from looking in on Ms. Jordon."

"What can you tell me, Dr. Lee?"

"I'm afraid there isn't much I can say. There has been no change in her condition since she was brought into the hospital. I'm sorry to say the prognosis is getting worse. The longer she stays in this state, the less likely she is to recover. On the other hand, she could come out of the coma any moment. It is impossible to say."

"I must ask, Mr. Williams, do you know if Ms. Jordon has a Living Will? It might come to the point where a decision must be made concerning continuation of life support. I know it is not pleasant to talk about these things. It has been my experience, however, that loved ones should be prepared for the worst and hope for the best. If a life support decision is required, there needs to be either a Living Will or a next of kin. In the case of neither, I'm afraid the courts will have to get involved."

"The only relative she has," said Ethan, is her mother, who is in a nursing home with dementia."

"If there is no Living Will," Dr. Lee said, "the Court can appoint a guardian of person, perhaps you. If I can be of any help, please give me a call. Good-bye, Mr. Williams."

Damn him, Ethan thought. He talks like she's already dead. Well, the hell with him. I'm not about to give up. Ethan then called Harold.

"Harold, I want to apologize for my attitude this morning. I was pretty upset over Beth and wasn't feeling too well myself.

"I know, but I'm under pressure to get results.

"Be assured that I'll be back on your case tomorrow."

"Good."

"I'll call you periodically to keep you up on the status, Ethan told him. In the meantime, you can at least tell your brother and sister that I'm working."

"Okay," Harold said, and hung up.

Ethan went back to Beth's room. She was positioned slightly more to the left than she had been when he left her earlier. He sat down beside the bed, pushed the red curls back from her forehead, and took her hand in his. He looked at her closed eyes and remembered what the doctor had said about talking to someone in a coma. Not knowing what else to say, he recited nursery rhymes. "Mary had a little lamb; its fleece was white as snow, everywhere that Mary went, the little lamb was sure to go. Hickory, dickory, dock, the mouse ran up the clock, The clock struck one —, ...three blind mice —, ...the mouse ran up the clock — ...They all ran after the Farmer's wife, three blind mice." As Ethan said the last word, he felt a slight sensation on his hand and looked down. He thought he felt it again. "Oh, my God!" he said. He looked back at her face, and he saw it.

CHAPTER TWELVE

"Doctor Lee, I tell you she moved her hand and her eyes."

"That's wonderful, Mr. Williams, but sometimes, there are involuntary muscle spasms. We will take her to an examining room and run some tests. Then we will know for sure. He asked Ethan to stand back while the orderly rolled the bed from the room.

Ethan was waiting for the report on Beth. It had been two and a half hours since they went off for the examination and testing. Just as he returned from across the room for coffee, the doctor walked in.

"Mr. Williams, I'm sorry to have kept you waiting so long but we wanted to be sure. I have good news. Ms Jordon has started to come out of the coma. She's not awake yet, but she shows neurological response and has opened and closed her eyes. There is no sign that she is able to see, but I think it is just a matter of time."

"Can I go in?"

"Yes, whenever you like."

Ethan met the nurse on his way back to Beth's room. "You'll have to say good night, Mr. Williams, Visiting hours are over.

"Nurse, can't you make an exception? She's coming out of the coma.

"She smiled at Ethan and said, "Isn't it wonderful? Don't tell anyone I broke the rule, go on in."

"Hi Beth" he said, as he took hold of her hand. She turned her head ever so slightly towards him, but her eyes remained closed.

He kissed her. He felt her hand tighten, almost imperceptibly. "Beth darling, I love you so much and I know you're going to pull through this. I'm so anxious to look at you eye-to-eye and have a real conversation that I can hardly stand it. I have to go now but I'll be back to tomorrow. He leaned over and kissed her one more time.

The elation of Beth's improvement caused Ethan to forget everything else. As he was leaving the hospital to head for his car, He realized it was approaching six o'clock and his back was hurting. He'd go back to the motel, remove the brace, take a pill, shower, then put the brace back on and get something to eat before turning in.

He woke up Monday morning feeling pretty good. He rested over the weekend except for visiting Beth. She appeared to be getting stronger and more responsive each day. The doctor said it would take quite a while for her to get back to normal, although he said she might open her eyes and, or talk any day. Ethan was very anxious.

With Beth improving, Ethan thought he should try to get a little work done. It was a beautiful day. It was cold and the sun was shinning through the large window in his room. He showered and went out for breakfast.

After eating, he headed for Eastern Avenue and the address that Beth had given him for Rebecca Stone. He parked in front, climbed the steps of the small stoop, and knocked. The door opened a couple of inches exposing an interior that was pitch black. An elderly lady said in a raspy voice "Yes?"

"I'm looking for a Rebecca Stone."

"Who are you?"

"Private Investigator."

"How do I know?"

He showed her his license.

"She doesn't live here any more."

"Do you know where she lives now?"

"No"

"Does anyone around here know?"

"You might ask at the bar around the corner," She pointed to her left"Thank." Ethan walked down the steps and to the corner.

'HAP'S BAR' was painted on the window above a Miller's beer sign.

He entered to see a long narrow bar stretched out to his right. There was a tall thin white haired man standing at the end of the bar facing him as he entered. There were about six customers hunched over the bar nursing beers.

"Hi, Mister," he said, "My name's Hap, what can I get you?"

"I'm looking for some information," Ethan said. "Do you know Rebecca Stone?"

"Sure, she lived around the corner for ten, maybe twelve years."

"Do you know where she lives now?"

"No, but I heard she went into a nursing home a while back. I don't know which one. You might ask one her old neighbors, Bill Randolph on this side of where she used to live or Doris King on the other side.

"Thanks Hap, for your help."

"Any time."

He went to the Randolph's and the King's. Randolph confirmed that Rebecca went to a nursing home but he didn't know which one. He also confirmed that she had a daughter whose name he couldn't remember. Doris King wasn't home.

He stood on the sidewalk in front King's house for a moment thinking about what he should do next. He decided to go see Beth. He pulled a notebook from his pocket and made a notation of the time he'd spent working on the case so far that day. He then closed the book, put it in his pocket and headed for his car. He sat in the car for a while to give his back a rest.

Before Ethan got to the hospital a freezing rain had started. Shit, he thought, here it is late march and we get freezing rain. I can't believe it. He took his time because the roads were starting to get slippery. He parked the car as close to the hospital as possible and walked very carefully to the door. All he needed was to fall and fracture his back again.

The nurses at the station gave him big hellos and smiles as he approached. He stopped and asked how Beth was doing.

"She's doing better," one of the nurses said, "she's been opened her eyes this morning. We're going to try giving her some liquids this morning to see if she will respond to a spoon and be able to swallow. It will probably take a while and wear her out. I think it would be best if you would come back this afternoon."

In order to kill time until he could visit Beth again, Ethan ate lunch and went back to Eastern Avenue to visit Doris King. This time he took a route past the south end of Patterson Park. The park is a nine square block area of green grass and trees in the middle of a concrete jungle of streets and row homes slowly turning commercial. It had always been a playground for children and pets alike. Today, the ground as well as the trees is covered with ice, making the park look like a winter wonderland. Turning left onto Eastern at the south end of the park, Ethan was still thinking about the nurse trying to give Beth liquids from a spoon. It was a very encouraging sign,

He was able to park directly in front of King's house. He went to the door and knocked several times before he got an answer. "Hi," he said, with his ID in sight.

The attractive blond woman that opened the door said, "May I help you?"

I'm a private investigator, and I'm looking for Rebecca Stone. Mr. Randolph said you might be able to help. I know she's in a nursing home. Do you know which one?"

"I don't know. You see I was away on vacation and when I came back she was gone and the house was up for sale."

"Did she ever say anything to you about a child?"

"We never talked much, but one time she did mention a daughter in passing. She didn't give any details and I never asked. I'm sorry I can't help."

Yeah, right. He said, "Thanks."

Ethan couldn't have felt lower if he was a snake. His head was down and his chin was against his chest. He thought he would do a lot better with the address lead that Beth had given him. As things stood on the Farnsworth case, he was still at the beginning. The only thing he knew for sure was that Rebecca Stone was in a nursing home, had a daughter, and was senile. What a roaring start. He recorded his time and headed back to the motel.

CHAPTER THIRTEEN

In Syracuse, Harold was discussing Ethan's progress with his brother and sister.

"Whadaya expect me to, George? Ethan called and said he's in Baltimore to work on our case, but there's a problem." Harold explained about the accidents and said, "I pressured him, but geez, there's a limit to what I can do."

"Why the hell don't you get somebody else?" George yelled.

"Because, he told me he'd start working the case. He also said he'd only bill us for time he actually worked."

"Boy, that's kind of him," George said, not hiding his sarcasm. "I still think you should get somebody else."

"It'd be stupid to start all over. The guy's up against it right now. We need to cut him a little slack. It's my decision to make, and I'm giving him a chance to do the job I hired him for."

"Well you had better stay on top of it and get some results. 'Cause Linda and me need the goddamn money, and fast!"

"Yeah," Joyce agreed, meekly, "we need the money too."

"Well, I'm sorry you guys are so damn anxious, but I'm the executor, and I'll decide when it's released. If you're not happy with the way things are going, talk to Charles Boynton. He'll tell you that the Will gives me, and no one else, total responsibility and authority in the matter."

"Yeah, but—"

Harold interrupted. "I don't see any reason to continue this meeting. I'll call you when I get something further."

George was leaning back in his chair, with his feet propped up on a partially open drawer, reading the paper, when the phone rang. He put his feet down and picked it up. "Hello. David! How are you?" he said in a lighthearted tone.

David Wilson had just gotten back to his small office in the rear of his pizza shop after getting the mail. Sorting the junk from the important stuff, he suddenly stopped and dropped everything except the letter he held in his hand. He had just torn it open to find it was from the Internal Revenue Service.

"Don't 'How are you?' me, you incompetent bastard! I just got another letter from the goddamn IRS. This is the third one in five years. This time, the damn bill's over five thousand dollars!"

"Calm down, David," Farnsworth said, interrupting him. "I'm sure it's some kind of mistake. I'll take care of it."

"Calm down my ass! You're goddamn right you'll take care of it, and you'll never do another tax return for me again!" Shouted Wilson.

"I'll be right over for the letter, and get on it immediately," George countered.

"You'll get on it all right, and I meant what I just said. After this episode, you are through as my accountant!"

Linda Farnsworth was not in good physical shape. George worked out in a gym three times a week, but Linda sat around and munched on snacks and watched TV if she wasn't out to lunch or playing bridge with her friends. When George called, she was in the middle of a bagel with cream cheese and jelly, watching Regis and Kelly.

"Hi George, whacha want?" She took a bite of bagel.

"I just got a call from David Wilson, and he canceled his account."

"Which one's Wilson?" she asked.

"He's the one who owns the pizza shop. I also do his personal taxes."

"George, that's a pretty big job, and it's the third one you've lost since August." She sounded worried.

"I know. And our bills are eating us alive. If we don't get that inheritance soon, we're going to really be in trouble. I don't know how much longer we can keep our heads above water."

"Well, George, you're just going to have to get more clients to keep us going until we get that money."

"Yeah, right; you talk like it's easy. I have enough trouble keeping the ones I've got. It may boil down to you having to get a job."

"I'll tell you one thing, George, that's not an option, because I don't have time."

George hung up and headed for his favorite bar.

The double doors were frosted glass. A lighted shade hanging over the doors was labeled BRASS RAIL. Inside, the bar stretched straight back along the right wall. The place was packed, noisy, and smelled of smoke and stale beer. The bartender was standing in front of George as he polished glasses. He set the glass he was working on down, and poured George another gin and tonic. "George, That's your fourth in two hours. You had better slow down.

"I tell you, Arthur," George said, "I don't know how a man is supposed to get ahead these days. Everything I make goes to bills. My wife doesn't have a clue. All she does is set around the house, or go out and spend money. Then she gives me hell because I don't make enough."

If I mention she should help out, she refuses. You'd think she'd want to help out some. My father passed away, bless his soul, and I'm supposed to inherit some money, but my goddamned fat-assed brother is executor of the Will, and is dragging his feet without a bit of concern for my financial situation." He drained his glass and said, "Gimme another."

"This is your last drink," Arthur said. "You're drunk, George, how about me calling you a cab?"

"I don't need a cab." He teetered on the stool, gave his glass a push, brushed his nose with the back of his hand and said, "Fill'er up."

CHAPTER FOURTEEN

The nurse on duty told Ethan that Beth had been awake for a while after he had left the day before. It was nine o'clock in the morning now, and she was still sleeping. Ethan sat by the bed holding her hand for about an hour when suddenly her hand tighten on his and her eyes opened. "Beth, it's Ethan; can you see, and hear me?" He thought she smiled slightly.

"Oh my God! Can you talk?" Her lips parted, but no sound came out. Tears spilled down his cheeks, as he began to sob. He held her hand and continued to cry while laying his head on her arm.

Ethan sat with Beth until she went to sleep. Pushing his chair back, and feeling completely drained, he put his elbows on his knees and his head in his hands. He tried to sort out in his mind exactly what he had experienced. Beth squeezing his hand, ever so slightly, but she had squeezed it. He thought she had smiled after he spoke to her. Had she, or was it just wishful thinking on his part? Then, did she open her mouth and try to talk? Was that effort in response to his speaking to her? Ethan was indeed, emotionally and physically exhausted, and wanted desperately to talk to Dr. Lee.

Ethan looked at Beth sitting along side him in the convertible as they were riding along the Chesapeake Bay. Her long, red hair was blowing in all directions. Beth was looking at him and smiling as she opened her mouth to say something.

He awoke when someone shook him by the shoulder. "Uh, what?" he murmured half asleep.

"It's Dr. Lee."

"Oh, yeah, must have fallen asleep," Ethan said, as he sat up, rubbing his eyes.

"It's all right, I know the stress you're under. Let's go down the hall and talk."

The rest area wasn't fancy, but it was private. Dr. Lee said, "I checked on Ms. Jordon before coming here. Her eyes were open, and she made some movements including her mouth and eyes. However, she was not able to make any verbal sounds. She is asleep now.

"I found the same thing when I was in her room a little while ago," Ethan responded, in a somewhat concerned voice.

"You may feel depressed by what you've seen today," Dr. Lee said, "But, actually, you should be encouraged. She has made remarkable progress and the first step to recovery. The next major event that we should see is her ability to make verbal sounds. There is no way to know how long it will take for her to speak. If you need me, just let the nurses know."

At, 1:30, Ethan left the hospital. He would have stayed longer but besides only allowing relatives to visit, there were specific hours for visiting. Not being able to stay with Beth, Ethan found doing some work helped relieve his stress. This afternoon, he would again tackle the task of finding Rebecca Stone. He knew now for sure that she was in a nursing home.

Ethan went back to the motel and got out the Yellow Pages. The size of the book was intimidating. Opening the book to the N's, he found two to three pages of nursing homes. Obviously, it would be a very laborious task to call them all. It would be worth the effort to try to find some other way. He sat back and thought how the job might be made easier. The nursing home list could be narrowed considerably by assuming she would go to one not far from where she had lived. That was definitely an option. Another was going to city hall to look up the property history in order to find out who handled the most recent sale. Through the realtor, he might find out where Rebecca went. He decided to try the first option and sat down at the desk to dial a number.

"Hello, Chuck, it's Ethan."

"How are you feeling?" Chuck asked.

"Pretty good. Every day I feel a little better."

"How about Beth?"

"She's improving, too, but it's very slow. She has periods each day now, when she's awake and exhibiting some motion.   But Beth still hasn't made any verbal sounds. The doctor is very encouraged though, and says it will now just take time. Chuck, you said if I needed help to give you a call. Is the offer still open?"

"Of course, what can I do?"

"The person I'm looking for is in a nursing home and there must be twenty or more of them. I thought you might have someone who knows the city well enough to identify the homes listed in the phone book that are closest to her old address."

"I have just the man. When do you need it?"

"Yesterday. Sooner would be better."

"How about five-thirty?"

"I'll be there," Ethan said

Ethan arrived at police headquarters at 5:20. "Hey, Chuck. Where do we stand?"

"I've got some information for you. Walt, that's the guy I had look into the nursing home thing, said there are only four homes within two miles. There's not much chance there. Better news, though, there are twelve within ten miles. I think the twelve will give you some chance of finding what you want."

"I agree," Ethan said. "I owe you."

"Not yet. If you find what you're looking for, then you owe me."

"Fair enough."

Chuck said, "Here's the list, and you're welcome to use a phone and desk here to follow up, if you like."

"Thanks for the offer, but I'm going to see Beth before I start working the list." They shook hands.

"Hi, Beth," he said, as he entered her room. She responded with a very slight smile. He hurried to her bedside, leaned over, and kissed her as he took her hand. "How are you today, Darling?" There was no response, but the attentive look and smile remained. "You look wonderful. Can you talk yet?" She opened her mouth slightly, but no sound came out. She seemed a little more alert, though, and a little stronger.

I shouldn't hope for too much too fast, he thought, but she's improved slightly since the last time I saw her. Thank God! "Beth, I'll stay here with you as long as they'll let me." He no sooner finished the sentence when the nurse came in and asked him to leave.

"I have to go now, Darling. You continue to get better, and I'll see you soon." He leaned over, and as he kissed her, felt a slight squeeze on his hand.

Back in his hotel room, he sat down at the desk with the list of names and phone numbers and went to work. The first eight numbers he called were strikeouts. His ninth call was to the Deaton Nursing Home. He had success! After identifying himself, Ethan told the administrator that he was a private investigator and needed to get in contact with Rebecca Stone concerning an inheritance. He was told they had had a patient by that name but the administrator said, "Mr. Williams, she is no longer here."

"Why not?" Ethan asked.

"Ms. Stone was taken to Mercy Hospital."

Ethan tapped his pen in nervous excitement. "How long will she be there?"

"I'm afraid she's not there any more."

"What do you mean?"

"Last week, shortly after Ms. Stone was taken to the hospital, she got pneumonia, and then had a heart attack. I'm sorry to say that she passed away and her daughter had the body cremated."

"Do you have any information on the daughter?" Ethan asked, hopeful that he was getting close to finding Harold's sibling.

"I can't give that information out over the phone. I'd have to see some identification," the lady said.

"All right," Ethan said, "I'll be right over."

The nursing home was on Eutaw and Mulberry Streets. It was in a decrepit brick building with stairs and a ramp leading up to half-glass doors. A guard sat at a metal desk reading a Ludlum paperback.

"May I help you?" he asked.

"I have an appointment with the administrator."

The guard gave him long and complicated instructions that a civil engineer would have had trouble following. Then, he handed him a map. Jerk, Ethan thought, why didn't he give me the damn map to begin with?

When he got to the desk, he said, "I'm here to see Ms. Bernardi."

"She's in the third office on the right," the dark haired receptionist said, pointing over her shoulder.

Ethan knocked on the glass door. "Ms Bernardi, I'm Ethan Williams."

"Come in. Have a seat. Let me see some identification." Ethan showed her his PI license. She studied it for a few minutes. "Rebecca Stone's daughter's name is Sara Stone," she told him.

"Do you know where she lives or works?"

"She works for Teeter Tot Toys."

"Where are they located?"

"In Perry Hall on Silver Spring Road." She said.

God, Ethan thought, this is ridiculous. Showing his exasperation with her stretching out the information, by noisily exhaling, he said, "Where's that?"

"Between Route 1 and Interstate 95, northeast of the city," she replied.

He left the Administration office and wound his way through the labyrinth of ramps, halls, doors, and steps, to the parking lot, and his car. After looking at a map, he headed out to Perry Hall.

About an hour later, Ethan reached TTT. He followed the signs, parked in the visitor's lot, and entered the building. He identified himself to the guard, and asked for Sara Stone.

"She doesn't work her anymore," he said.

"What do you mean?" Ethan asked. Damn, he thought, I'm chasing a ghost.

"Just what I said. She quit the company, and left yesterday."

"Where'd she go?

"I don't know. You could ask Personnel."

"Would you get them on the phone for me?" Ethan asked. The guard dialed the number and handed him the phone.

"I'm trying to contact Sara Stone, and I understand she has left your company."

"Yes, she has."

"Could you give me a forwarding address for her?"

"I'm afraid I don't have one," the woman said. "Even if I did, I wouldn't be allowed to give it out. Company policy."

"Who can make an exception to company policy?" was Ethan's next question.

"You'd have to talk to our President and CEO, Mr. Johnson. Sara reported to him, and he might know where she went. He also, controls Company Policy."

Ethan hung up, turned to the guard, and said, "Can you get Johnson on the phone for me.

"No, but I can get his secretary."

"Okay."

"Mr. Johnson's office," a pleasant female voice announced.

"This is Ethan Williams calling. May I speak to Mr. Johnson?"

"Mr. Johnson's not in the office today. Would you like to leave a message?" He told her why he wanted to see Johnson, and asked for an appointment. "It seems that around every turn is a wall," he muttered, as he left the lobby.

CHAPTER FIFTEEN

On the way back from TTT, Ethan thought about how little progress he'd made since he started the Farnsworth case. He knew he was looking for a female named Sara Stone. Not much progress to show for over two month's work. Maybe his appointment with Johnson on Thursday would give him a lead. He was going to see Beth on the way back to the motel, so he swung west and went down Route 1 where he found a diner along the way, and stopped for lunch.

As Ethan entered it, he thought, what a dive! Either the owner hasn't heard about the dangers of secondhand smoke or doesn't care. He ignored the surroundings, took a seat at the counter, and ordered coffee. When the waitress came back he said, "I'll have a hot roast beef sandwich and French fries with gravy on both." Ethan didn't worry about the greasy food anymore since the doctor put him on Pravachol to control his cholesterol. He figured what the hell, if I have to take a pill, I might as well enjoy life.

After lunch, he went to see Beth. She was sitting up in bed and appeared bright. As in the past few visits, she looked at him and smiled. Ethan waved and said "Hi, Beth." He thought he saw the blanket move and wondered if she had tried to wave back. He quickly walked over to the bed, reached under the blanket and took hold of her hand. "I love you," he said, leaning over and kissing her on the lips. He thought he felt her respond slightly. Was he imagining things?

"Beth, you're making progress; at least I hope so, Darling."

As he was about to sit down along side the bed, Dr. Lee walked in. "Mr. Williams, how nice to see you," he said, taking two long steps to reach Ethan as he extended his hand.

"Hi, Dr. Lee. How's Beth doing?"

"We ran tests this morning and they showed that the healing process is coming along nicely. The internal swelling, although not completely gone, has reduced considerably. That accounts for her increased alertness and responsiveness. I believe she will fully recover. It's just a matter of time."

"How is your back, Mr. Williams?"

"Okay," Ethan said. "I keep the brace on except for showering and sleeping. It gets tired during the day and hurts some, but nothing I can't deal with."

Dr. Lee said, "I had a call from your Dr. Cook at Mercy Hospital in Scranton yesterday. He asked if I could arrange for X-rays to be taken here, since it's been a little over two months since your accident. I can arrange that through one of our orthopedic doctors here at the hospital, and he will send a report to Dr. Cook."

"That would be fine, Ethan said."

"Check with the nurse on duty tomorrow for details on the arrangements," the doctor said as he left.

Ethan thought it was time to call Harold to give him a status report.

"Hi, Harold; it's Ethan."

"So, how's it going?"

"Very slow, but I thought I should fill you in on where we stand. I know I promised you weekly reports, and normally I would do that for clients. This case, though, is quite different from normal. I've been plagued with problems from the beginning. I started out with practically no leads. Your family was unfriendly, and of absolutely no help. Then, Beth and I had the accidents, which delayed progress. When I finally got started, nearly every major lead has turned out to be a dead end. Therefore, I apologize that this is only the third time I've reported to you. But with things the way they've been, the accidents coupled with the progress to date, reports just weren't warranted."

"I'm getting a lotta pressure from George and Joyce," Harold said. "You need to speed things up."

"I'm going as fast as I can," Ethan said, thinking about his own pressures. Harold was pressuring him because he didn't have the gumption to stand up to his brother and sister. Ethan was feeling tremendous pressure, fear and frustration of his own because of Beth's condition. He said, "I'm sorry, Harold, but you have to deal with your brother and sister. As I told you before, if you're not satisfied, you can get someone else. However, from what I've found out so far, it won't do you any good to change investigators.

Your sibling is a female, and her name is Sara Stone. I located her mother, but she has passed away. Now, I'm following up on where she worked. That's where we stand at the moment. I know it's not much. Because progress is so slow, I'll continue to give you telephone reports rather than take the time to prepare written ones. Do you have a problem with that?"

"No."

"Good, then that's the way we'll leave it for now and I'll call you each time I have something to report. In the meantime, don't let your brother and sister browbeat you."

Harold called the family bi-weekly meeting at a restaurant instead of his home. He thought being in a public place might ease the tension, and everyone could have a drink, the cost of which would be included in the expenses associated with settlement of the estate. In addition, a drink might give him more courage to stand up to his brother and sister. He was wrong.

The meeting had just gotten under way. Harold began to explain the report he had just received from Ethan, when George raised his voice, slapped the table, and said, "Goddamn it, Harold, you're too easy on this Williams guy! You'd think he was paying you, the way you're letting him drag his feet on this thing!"

"I don't agree, George; I think he's doing well considering the circumstances. He had no information to start with, and then, there were the devastating accidents.

During those same two months, he found out that we have a sister whose name is Sara Stone," Harold said.

"La-de-da," Joyce said. He's put us one step closer to losing a quarter of our inheritance, not to mention the million you'll get if she's found."

"That's right," George chimed in.

"You guys are too much," Harold said. "First, you say I'm not pushing hard enough on the case, and then you say that I'm the only one with something to gain if she's found. Both of you can go to hell! I'm in charge of the investigation, and I'll run it the way I damn well please regardless of what you think!" He finished his drink, slammed the glass down, stood, and said, "This meeting is over." He threw money on the table for the drinks and left."

Joyce and George didn't move.

George was the first to speak. "You know, Joyce, if we could find this woman before Harold does, and get rid of her, we could each gain a third more of a quarter of the estate. That's a lot of money. I talked to the lawyer, Boynton, last week, and he estimates the estate to be worth about twenty four million. If this Sara wasn't in the picture, you and I would each get about two million more."

"George, what are you saying?"

"I'm saying I think we should hire our own private investigator to find Sara Stone, and then find some way to cut her out."

"And just how do you plan to accomplish that, dear brother?"

"I have to think about that," he said.

"George, I'm not going to sit here and listen to your stupid alcoholic talk. Besides, I have to go. John will be getting home soon and he'll expect dinner to be ready." She got up to leave. George stood, too, and headed for the bar.

CHAPTER SIXTEEN

After getting his dreaded call to Harold out of the way, Ethan headed for the hospital.

The nurse at the station on Beth's floor said, "Mr. Williams, Dr. Lee has arranged for your X-rays at 9:00 down in radiology on the ground floor. Dr. Brooks in orthopedics will let me know when he has read the films, and when you can see him for a consultation."

With some anxiety, Ethan did as he was told. He found X-ray and had to wait a short while before he was called in. The young technician asked him to remove his shirt and brace before taking the X-rays. It was only a few minutes before he came out and told Ethan that the films all looked acceptable and he could go.

Ethan went back upstairs to see Beth. Stopping at her room, he looked in. She was propped up in bed facing the TV. He knocked lightly at the open door. Walking to the bed, he said, "Hi, Beth." For the first time, before he could reach down and take her hand, she reached out slightly towards his. Ethan grinned, and said, "Beth, darling, that's wonderful!" She just maintained her smile and looked straight ahead. He leaned down and gave her a long intimate kiss on the lips. He thought he felt a slight response, but couldn't be sure. Before he could stand up, her hand went limp, and she was asleep. He quietly left the room and stopping at the station to tell the nurse what had happened. She said, "Don't get discouraged, Mr. Williams, she probably just got tired. It's best to let her sleep now." Ethan nodded and left with a sad expression on his face.

It had been a stressful day, and he anticipated another one tomorrow when he would see Johnson at Teeter Tot Toys. He stopped in the motel bar for a drink before going to his room.

After his brace was off, he laid down on the bed for a few minutes before showering, just looking up at the smoke detector. He'd been in this room for about two months, and the walls were beginning to close in. Hopefully, he and Beth would both get better soon and back to their normal lives.

"That was a wonderful dinner, Ethan," Beth said.

"Now for the dessert," he said, as he laid a gray velour box on the table in front of her. "Oh-h-h!" she said, putting her hand over her mouth. The diamond was emerald-cut and a half-carat, set in a white gold mounting. Beth smiled while looking at the ring, too thrilled for words. She got out of her chair, went around the table, and gave Ethan a kiss, ignoring that they were in a restaurant. After sitting down, she said,"Let's set the date for two weeks from today and leave for Syracuse tomorrow! She then rose once more, went around the table again, gave him another kiss and said, "I love you!"

Ethan was disappointed when he woke up. He thought they were getting on with the rest of their lives, and then realized he had been dreaming. Looking at his watch, and seeing that it was six o'clock, Ethan was amazed that he had slept almost three hours. He sat up carefully and prepared to take his shower. After cleaning up, putting on his brace and getting dressed, he went out to get pizza.

The next morning, after breakfast, he headed for TTT. He told the guard in the lobby that he had an appointment with Jeff Johnson. The man placed a call and said, "Mr. Johnson is expecting you. Go through the door and turn right. His office is at the end of the hall."

Then he pushed a buzzer releasing the latch on the entrance. Going through the door, Ethan was impressed. The paintings were obviously originals, the paneling walnut, and the carpeting very expensive. Heading down the hall he noticed all the titles and names on the office doors. On entering the door marked 'Johnson', the secretary said, "Go right in, Mr. Williams."

Johnson stood as he entered and came around the desk to shake hands. Ethan showed him his credentials and told him what he wanted. "Yes, Mr. Williams, Personnel explained the purpose of your visit. I'm sorry to say, however, that you're too late. Sara quit last Friday, and I don't know where she went."

"Isn't that odd?" Ethan asked, "Didn't she work for you in an important capacity?"

"Yes, to both questions," he said. "Normally in the case of an employee with Sara's position and status, there would be a separation package and an amicable parting. In such a case, I would know where she went. In this situation, however, her leaving was not friendly. Sara and I had a very severe disagreement over matters of business practices. There were compelling reasons for the disagreement, which I can't go into. Since she was vice president in charge of operations, I out-ranked her as President and CEO. Consequently, we reached an impasse. She quit, and without warning, and was gone the next day. I have no idea where she went or what she plans to do. I tried to reason with her and failed. The company will miss her."

"Personnel also told me that you'd like her home address. It's not our policy to give out that kind of information, but because of the unusual circumstances here, I'm going to make an exception. I've instructed my secretary to have the address ready when you leave. I'm sorry the situation is what it is, and that I can't be of further help." He punched the intercom button. "Claire, Mr. Williams is ready to leave."

"I appreciate the address, Mr. Johnson," Ethan said. Claire opened the door, and Ethan followed her out. She handed him a slip of paper. He thanked her, left the building, and headed for his car with Sara's address in hand.

The Regency apartment building was five stories, brick and located in an exclusive section of Towson. The directory in the lobby listed Sara Stone on the third floor, apartment 342. Ethan dialed the number. There was no answer. He tried it again and let it ring longer. There was still no answer. Looking at the list again, he saw one marked 'Superintendent, 001'and dialed it. After a few seconds, a gruff voice said, "This is the Superintendent."

"I'm looking for Sara Stone."

"I won't bother asking who you are, because she's not here."

"Do you know when she'll be back?"

"She won't."

"What do you mean?"

"She moved out."

"Did she leave a forwarding address?"

"Nope. Sara settled her rent late Friday telling me that the stress at work had become too much, and it was time to leave. She put her clothes and personal belongings in the car and said, "I'll send for the rest later," and then drove off.

"That's it? She just left, no indication of where she was going or what she was going to do?"

"That's it."

"Shit," Ethan said. "I can't believe this." He turned and headed back to his car.

It was late afternoon the previous Thursday when Sara stormed into Jeff Johnson's office. "Jeff," she said, "I'm tired of all the shit I've taken from you during the last three years!"

"Whoa, Sara, what's wrong?"

She waved the recall plan in his face. "This plan I put together is the latest example. I work my ass off, with the help of the rest of the staff, to develop a plan in the ridiculously short time that you gave us. We did an incredible job developing a plan that provides a recall, the speed of which is mind-boggling. You hardly look at it, reject it, and then put the heat back on me to go do the impossible."

"Sara," he interrupted, "sometimes it's necessary —

She cut him off and continued, "All this pressure for a problem that's not my fault and, in fact, is more your fault than anyone's. The rest of the staff and I come up with suggestions and advice that you reject outright without consideration, override recklessly, or just plain ignore. As a result, we get into messes like the one we're in now. The reason this happened is because you wouldn't allow one hundred percent lot sampling on the material as we requested. We told you that an AQL inspection on this type material was dangerous. Just like the lead in the game pieces on the previous problem, and the acidic dye on the play money before that. I feel I've got a thankless job, and I'm tired of bailing your ass out of trouble! I think it's only a matter of time before you pull this company under. I'm cleaning my desk out tomorrow and leaving.

"Sara, you can't be serious. You're a key player in this company and have a great future here."

"Forget it, Jeff, it's too late." She slammed the door as she left the office.

CHAPTER SEVENTEEN

As Ethan drove away from Sara's apartment building, he told himself that she was probably distraught by the loss of her mother, and having no other relatives, decided to get away to make a fresh start. It's not unusual for a person holding a high position such as hers to not have many close friends. The hard thing now was to determine what the next step should be. It was a long shot, but he would give Jeff Johnson another call.

"Hello, Mr. Williams, what can I do for you?"
"Mr. Johnson, I'm still trying to find Sara Stone. She's moved out of her apartment and left no forwarding address. I've tried the phone company, the power company, the DMV, her childhood neighborhood, and her neighbors in the apartment house she just moved out of. It's almost like

she doesn't want anyone to know where she is. The reason I called you again is to ask you if she was especially friendly with any particular colleague or colleagues there at TTT."

"There were two members of my staff with whom Sara seemed to be fairly friendly: Mark Hefron, V.P. of Finance, and Herm Henderson, V.P. of Quality. You could try anyone on my staff, but I think those two are your best bet. My secretary can give you a complete list of names and extensions."

Later, when Ethan called Johnson's office from his car, the pleasant voice of his secretary said, "Hi, Mr. Williams. It's nice to talk to you again. Mr. Johnsion just asked me to give you a list of names. Can you stop by and pick it up?"

"Yes, I'm in my car and not far away and If it's okay, I'll drop by now."

"That'll be fine."

Ethan made a U-turn, picked up the list from Claire Roberts and went on his way.

Sara wondered if she had acted foolishly in quitting her job without having something else firmed up. It was probably even more foolish not to have negotiated some kind of severance package. On the other hand, she had had it with Johnson, and the adhesive problem was the last straw. Even if it would have been to her benefit to stay, she needed to be true to herself and to get away from him. As far as a job went, she wasn't worried. She was tired of working for the toy company even though she had a hi-level job that paid well. The company was very unstructured in the way it operated, which was largely due to the influence of Johnson. He really had the Board of Directors fooled. SEC, where she worked prior to TTT, on the other hand, was just the opposite. It was an aerospace company that followed very rigid rules. She liked that.

While she worked at there, a small company in Rochester, Ramax Microelectronics, had approached her. They manufactured thick film hybrid circuits for the military industry. At the time, they were a small start-up company, and had offered her a job with a stock option. The stock option was small. She thought at the time that her career would best be served by joining a more mature and larger company. Now she felt differently. Her career was firmly established, and she was financially comfortable.

She called Ramax before she had the confrontation with Johnson to explore the possibility of their still having an interest in her joining the company, and was surprised at their exuberance over her call. Not only did the president want to talk, but also was still willing to consider the offer of a stock option. When her plane landed in Rochester, she would stay at the Hampton Inn and go for an interview the next day.

The plane was being slammed up and down and back and forth sideways by the turbulence as they made their final approach for landing. The stewardess came on the PA system and said, "Ladies, and Gentlemen, we apologize for the bumpy ride, but I assure you that we will have a smooth landing."

Yeah, right, Sara thought as she tightened her seatbelt in anticipation of a smack-down landing. To her amazement, the pilot brought the plane very gently down on the runway even though, only seconds before touchdown, the nose of the plane was jerked sideways by the wind. Though it was a white knuckle landing, she remembered that an old pilot once told her that any landing you can walk away from is a good one. She wound her way to the baggage claim, retrieved her bag, and went to the Hertz counter. She signed the contract and got directions to the motel and Ramax. Then, she went outside to wait for the Hertz shuttle.

"What do you mean you don't have a room for me?" Sara said to the Hampton Inn clerk. "Teeter Tot Toys Corporate Headquarters made the reservation almost a week ago, and I have a conformation number. If you expect any more business from TTT, you'd better honor my reservation." They don't know I quit, she thought.

"Let me double check, Ms. Stone." The clerk disappeared through a door behind the counter. After a few minutes, a short man with bushy hair came out and said, "Ms. Stone, I'm the manager, and I want to apologize for the mix-up. Of course, we have a reservation for you. We have precisely what you requested, a no-smoking room, with a king-size bed. And for the inconvenience of the reservation mix-up, there will be no charge for the room. Here, at Hampton Inn, we guarantee total satisfaction." Yeah, Sara thought, especially when a corporation is mentioned.

Back at his motel, Ethan picked up the telephone to make a call when his cell phone rang. "Hello. Yes, Dr. Lee, Oh my god! That's wonderful news! I'll be right over." He closed the phone, grabbed his coat and raced out of the room, forgetting about the lingering pain in his back.

Ethan almost ran down the hall to Beth's room without even slowing down at the nurse's station. She turned her head and looked at him with a smile. Then, in a quiet, broken and hesitant voice she said, "H . . i E . . th . . n"

"Oh, Beth," he said, as he hurried to her bedside. He took her in his arms and they both cried. Dr. Lee was standing on the other side of the bed with a smile on his face enjoying the scene very much.

"I'll wait outside for you, Mr. Williams."

Ethan held her and kissed her. He stroked her hair and kissed her and kissed her. He told her over and over how much he loved her. The only other thing she tried to say was "Lo..v..." Then she closed her eyes. Ethan laid her head back on the pillow and she was asleep almost immediately.

"My god, Doctor," Ethan said, "does this mean she's well?"

"Not quite. She will have to go through quite a bit of speech and physical therapy. We'll start tomorrow with the speech therapy at a very slow pace, and then we will start the physical therapy."

"I'll wait as long as it takes," Ethan said. "The important thing is, she's making progress."

After spending as much time with Beth as they allowed, Ethan made his call to Herm Henderson. When he got through, he identified himself to the secretary, and told her

104

what he wanted. She apologized, telling him that Mr. Henderson would be out of town until late Tuesday, so Ethan made an appointment for Wednesday at nine.

Next, he tried Mark Hefron. The secretary answered and he went through the same ID-reason routine. "One moment. Let me check with Mr. Hefron." She came back on the line and said, "Mr. Hefron's day is full. The best he can do is talk over lunch."

"That would be great," Ethan said. "Where?"

"He suggested our cafeteria."

"Fine."

"Come to his office at 12."

Hefron's office was like Johnson's, only smaller. It had plush carpeting, walnut furniture, and watercolors on the walls.

"Mr. Williams, we can go straight to the cafeteria."

On the way, Hefron said, "I understand from my secretary that you want to talk about Sara Stone."

"That's right. I've been hired to find her and have run into a blind alley on every lead I've had, the last one being her job here at TTT. Jeff Johnson said he thought you and Ms. Stone were friends, and that you might be able to provide me with some help."

"What kind of help are you looking for?"

"No one seems to know where she is. I thought she may have said something to you that might give me a hint where to look. I can't betray the confidence of my client, but it's very important to him and to Ms. Stone that I find her."

"I saw Sara shortly before she left," Hefron said, "and she told me she hadn't been happy at TTT for some time. I think the final factor in her leaving was the death of her mother. If it hadn't been for her mother, she probably would have left some time ago."

"Did she tell you where she was going?"

"No, she said she'd call when she decided what she was going to do. It's my guess she'll call soon. Sara's not one to sit around with nothing to do."

"Will you call me if you hear from her?"

"I can't do that without her okay, but I will give her your message, name and number."

"Fair enough," he said handing Hefron his card. "My cell number's on there and I can be reached on it at any time." They rose together and Hefron walked Ethan to the lobby.

CHAPTER EIGHTEEN

George received his accounting degree in 1992. Instead of going to work for an established accounting firm, he started his own business. It was more impressive than working for someone else. In addition, he could set his own hours, which he did. He only worked when he felt like it. This made it hard for existing clients to reach him when they needed to, and he didn't work hard enough at getting new clients to increase the business base.

Then, there was his drinking problem. Put these things together, add in the tremendous debt that he and his wife Linda had created, and it became obvious why he was just hanging on by his fingernails. Receipt of the pending inheritance was of paramount importance to his financial survival. George called one of his clients, Nick Scalzi.

"Nick, I'd like to meet with you. I need your advice and help."

"What do you need, George?"

"I can't tell you over the phone. I'd like to meet with you in person."

"When do you want to meet and where?"

"Today at six o'clock in the Brass Rail."

"Pretty short notice, George."

"I know," but it's important."

"All right, I'll see you then."

Scalzi was responsive because George had been doing his taxes for a long time and had done a good job keeping his illegal business dealings away from the attention of the IRS.

Scalzi sat near the back of the dark bar. He nearly filled one side of the booth meant for two people. The scar on his right cheek stood out because of the light over the table. After greetings and ordering of drinks, George opened the conversation.

"Nick, I've been your accountant for how long, ten years? I've served you well. Right?"

"Yeah, yeah, what d'ya' want, George?"

"I need your help, Nick."

"Yeah, so you said on the phone. Spit it out."

"I need to find a woman and get rid of her. If you can help me, I'll make it worth your while."

"George, you've got a lotta balls. I don't do that kinda thing."

"I know, but I thought you might know somebody."

"All right, I can give you a name, but no guarantees. If he does it, it'll cost you double. Him and me."

"That's fine. Give me the name."

"His name is Orlando Secontini. You can get his number from the Yellow Pages. Secontini Construction. Tell him I told you to call." Without further discussion, George put money on the table for the drinks and left.

Back in the office, George ignored the blinking light on his answering machine and picked up the Yellow Pages, looked up Secontini's number, and placed the call.

"This is Secontini."

"Mr. Secontini, my name is George Farnsworth."

"Do I know you?"

"No, Nick Scalzi is a client of mine and he suggested I give you a call."

"Yeah? What do you want?"

"He thought you might help me with a problem I have. Could we meet somewhere to discuss it?"

"Yeah, since it's Scalzi. My office at three." He told George how to get there and hung up.

The Secontini construction office was a trailer set back from the road and surrounded by construction materials and equipment. George parked in the small lot in front of the trailer. He got out of the car, took the gravel path to the office, walking past a bulldozer, a pile of hot asphalt and a dump truck that looked like it hadn't been moved in several years. George knocked on the door and a voice he assumed was Secontini's, said, "Come on in."

Inside, Secontini was sitting at the desk on the right. He looked up, gray hair hanging down to his thick black eyebrows. He took a deep drag on his cigarette, causing his pockmarked cheeks to sink in. Inhaling, he said,

"Farnsworth, come on in and take a seat." He gestured to a chair at the end of his desk, and George did as he suggested.

"Now, what can I do for you?"

I'd like to have a person located and eliminated. Right now, there's a private investigator looking for her, too. I want her eliminated before he finds her. Do you think you can do it?"

"I can try. I normally wouldn't do this sort of job, but Scalzi's a good friend. If he wants me to help, then I'll help. Are you sure you can afford it?"

"The answer is yes, but there's an inheritance involved. We have to wait for the settlement of the will. That means finding the person I'm talking about, or waiting until it's determined that she can't be found, and the search is stopped. I don't want to wait. I want her found and removed from the picture. The sooner that happens the sooner payment can be made. I just need to know how much. I think there should be two numbers. One if your effort is successful, one if it's not, and the two numbers should be significantly different. I need to know what the numbers are before we agree."

"I'll be in touch before the end of the week," Secontini said.

Thursday, George was in his office when the telephone range. It was Secontini.

"I called Nick, and he says you're okay, so the numbers are 100 Grand if successful, 25 Grand if not, and a non-refundable deposit of 5 Grand, due before starting."

His hands shaking, George said, "That's acceptable. I'll drop off the 5 thousand tomorrow and give you the background information." After they hung up, Secontini made another call. "Kavichi, this is Secontini, I've got a job for you." I want you to hit a gal named Sara Stone. I don't know where she is or what she looks like. The only information I have is that a PI named Ethan Williams is looking for her too. If you stay on him, he should lead you to her. Keep me posted. He hung up without saying goodbye.

"Ethan, this is Harold. I'm really taking the heat from my brother and sister about your search. George wants your phone number and wants to know where you're staying."

"You tell George I work for you and any questions or comments he has can be directed to me through you. I know this might be difficult for you, but we can't let George take charge. If we do, it'll slow things down. I've found out where your sister worked. She's no longer there, but I may have a lead. I'll keep you informed."

"What kind of job did our sister have, Ethan?"

"She was Vice President of Operations for a company called Teeter Tot Toys."

"Wow!" Harold said. "That sounds like a pretty important job."

"It was. She reported to the President of the company. She quit last week, and so far, no one knows where she went. That's about it for now, Harold. I'll be in touch."

Bertrand Levitt sat in his office at Ramax Microelectronics in Irondequoit, New York, looking out at the evergreen trees, and tapping the eraser of his pencil on the top of the desk. He was contemplating the arrival of

Sara for her interview. Five years earlier, his Manager of Manufacturing had approached her while she worked at Scientific Electronics, and Levitt was very disappointed that she hadn't joined Ramax then.

He had talked to Sara a number of times at various corporate functions. Besides Levitt's own opinion of her capabilities, she was purported by many other corporate executives to have a strong will, good manufacturing, engineering, and quality skills, and a great way with people.

After she had recently called him to explore the possibility of joining the company, he had had a number of follow-up telephone conversations with her, which led him to feel certain she was the perfect candidate for President of Ramax Microelectronics. Also, he liked the idea of the company having a female corporate executive.

Sara entered the door to Levitt's office, and his secretary said, "Good morning, Ms. Stone. You may go right in. Mr. Levitt is expecting you."

Levitt rose as Sara entered and came around the desk. They exchanged greetings. He gestured to a chair by a coffee table and she sat down.

"Sara, from our discussions over the last month, and the two tours of the factory you've had, you know all about RMI and our need for a president. We've covered most of the questions on both your side and mine. I still have a couple of questions, however, before we get to the bottom line. Why do you want to leave TTT?"

"It's not 'want', it's 'did'."

"I don't understand."

"I quit TTT last Friday."

112

"That's a surprise. Why?"

"It's simple. Jeff Johnson and I couldn't agree on the way he was running the company. We disagreed for a long time on very basic issues that I was in no position to change. Since the situation hasn't improved over the years, I've been considering leaving for some time, so after my mother died recently, I saw no reason to postpone leaving."

"Can you elaborate on the issues?"

"Sure. He overrides quality control decisions, ignores sound engineering and manufacturing advice and, in my opinion, is leading the company towards a disaster."

Levitt smiled and asked, "Should I sell my stock?"

"I'm selling mine."

"What makes you think things won't be the same here?"

"RMI supports the military industry and, therefore, has more discipline and a set of rules that everyone must follow, including you and me, if I should get the job."

"I admire your candor and conviction to your principles. Why do you think you could handle this position, heading up a highly technical organization that builds military hardware, since you're coming from a commercial company?"

"Even though I've been working in a commercial operation," she said, "the job required control of manufacturing and interfacing with engineering, quality, reliability and finance organizations. A great deal of this work was technical in nature.

Before that, my experience at SEC was all technical. I don't see where any part of the job here would be an issue."

"Good," Levitt said, "I've been empowered by the Board of Directors to fill this position at my discretion. I'll tell you that the salary is two hundred fifty thousand with a year-end bonus of ten to fifteen percent, based on company performance. Also, the position includes a fifty thousand dollar stock option, redeemable over ten years. If you're interested, the job's yours," he said. "Just let me know when you can start."

"I'm very interested," she answered, "and I can start Monday."

"That's great, Sara," Levitt said, standing. I'll see you on Monday." They shook hands and Sara left.

CHAPTER NINETEEN

After accepting the job at RMI, Sara rented an apartment on the outskirts of Irondequoit where she had a view of a golf course, Irondequoit Bay, Lake Ontario, and a marina. She was sitting on her balcony looking at the spectacular view while she used her cell phone to make a call.

"Hi, Mark, this is Sara."

"Sara! It's great to hear your voice. Where are you?"

"I can't tell you, but I wanted you to know I've taken another job. I'm not telling where I am because I don't want Jeff to know. Over the last few years, he's gotten too used to leaning on me whenever he gets himself into trouble. Even though I've quit, if I know him, it won't keep him from calling. He didn't want me to quit and if he knows where I am, he'll badger me to come back. I don't want to have to deal with that. I didn't call to talk about him. I miss seeing you and hate not telling you where I am, but if you don't know, you won't have to lie."

"Sara, I'm glad to hear from you regardless. You can count on me not saying anything, but I hope we can keep in touch and go sailing again, soon."

"You can count on that as soon as I'm settled."

"That's great. By the way, a PI contacted me the other day, looking for you."

"Me? Why?"

"He wouldn't say, just that it's important to you."

"I'll say it again, Mark. I don't want anyone to know where I am. At least, not yet."

"Okay, Sara. If you change your mind and want to call him, he gave me his number."

"Okay, give it to me."

He gave her the number and she said, "I'll stay in touch, Mark. Bye."

The next morning, as Mark walked into his office, the telephone was ringing. He grabbed it and sat down. "Hello."

"Mr. Hefron, this is Ethan Williams. Have you heard from Sara?"

"She called, but wouldn't say where she is. I gave her your number. That's all I can do."

"Why won't she say where she is?" Ethan asked.

"I don't know. I guess she has her reasons."

"Okay. Thanks for giving her the message."

It was Friday, and, as usual, George had left the office early and gone to the Brass Rail. The place was full of smoke and crowded. George was sitting on his favorite stool at the end of the bar as he worked on his fourth gin and tonic. Arthur, the bartender, was standing with his back to him arranging bottles on one of the shelves in front of the large plate glass mirror behind the bar.

"Arthur, gimme another drink," George said.

"George, we go through this every night. You've had enough."

"Arthur, are you gonna give me a drink or do I have to go somewhere else?"

"All right, but this is the last one. Then I don't care where you go. But, you should go home, and if you'll let me, I'll call you a cab. I'll even pay for it." George didn't answer.

"Linda, I'm home. Where are you?"

"George, where the hell have you been? As if I didn't know. Do you know it's 8:30? What time did you leave work?"

Jeez, he thought, this sounds like twenty questions. He said, "Whoa, whoa, Darlin'." He staggered.

"Don't 'Darlin' me, you drunk"

"Now Linda, jus' cause I had a few drinks, don't mean I'm a drunk."

"Oh, yeah, what does it mean? It's not once in a while, George, it's every damn night, and I'm getting tired of it."

"Lindy, I have a couple a drinks at the end of the day to unwind. You know I have a very stressful job."

"Bullshit, George. You goof off all day and get drunk every night. That's why you can't keep the clients you have or get any new ones."

117

"You know, Linda, you're the main reason I go to the bar and have a few drinks rather than come home after work." He threw his hands up, staggered a bit, and said, "Aw, the hell with it. I'm going to bed." He swept his hands out and down like he was genuflecting, hitting Linda a glancing blow on the jaw. Not realizing what he had done, he staggered off to bed.

Linda, crying, picked up the phone and called her sister-in-law.
"Joyce, that brother of yours just hit me."
"He hit you? Oh my God!"
"Oh, I don't think he meant it." She sobbed. "But his drinking is out of control, and he's letting the business go down the tubes. The more I nag him, the worse things get. I don't know what to do." She continued to cry.
"Linda, calm down," Joyce said in a soothing voice. "I'll have John talk to him and see if he can help."

After another thirty minutes, Linda had calmed down considerably. She wiped her eyes and blew her nose. Then she said, "Thanks, Joyce. I don't know what I'd do if I didn't have you to talk to."
"Will you be okay now?" Joyce asked
"Yeah, he's in bed now. Usually, he goes to the office for a while on Saturday mornings if he's not too hung-over. Maybe John could talk to him then."
Joyce said, "I'll ask him tonight."
"Thanks," Linda said, still sniffling.
"You're welcome. Now calm yourself and try to get some rest tonight. When the private investigator finds our sister, and we get that inheritance, it will make everything

better. Then, things will work out, you'll see. I'll talk to you tomorrow. Bye."

"Bye, Joyce."

"John, I had a call from Linda tonight and she was in tears," Joyce said.

"What's wrong?"

"George is drunk again."

"Shit, he's always drunk."

"I know, but he is my brother, and Linda thinks it might help if you talk to him."

"Hell, Joyce, I've talked to him dozens of times. He always has excuses and denies he has a problem. He's an alcoholic, plain and simple, and needs help. I'm just not the right guy. George could probably go to AA and gain control, but it's easy for me to preach because I don't have the problem. Okay, I'll give him a call in the morning and try to go talk to him," John said.

Joyce moved up to her husband, put her arms around his neck, pressed her plump body against his, and gave him a big kiss. "John," she said, "I am so lucky to have you."

"Well, I don't know how lucky you are, but you're stuck with me." He smiled and kissed her again passionately.

Joyce said, "Shall we have dinner or…?"

"We can eat any time," he said as he took her hand.

CHAPTER TWENTY

After striking out with Hefron, Ethan thought he should call Harold.

"Harold, the last time we talked, I told you I had a lead to follow up on. It's still possible it could lead to something, but so far, nothing. And to be perfectly honest, I don't have high hopes."

"Damn it, Ethan, I'm up here, and you're down there. How do I know that you're even working on the case?"

"Harold, you don't. If you don't trust me, you damn well better get yourself another investigator. You know I've got problems. I'm in no mood for you to accuse me of cheating you. When I tell you that I'm doing everything possible on your case, I expect you to believe me. Is that clear, Harold?"

"Yes, Ethan."

"All right. Now, I've learned your sister doesn't want to be found. That makes the job extremely difficult and perhaps impossible. You'll have to decide if you want me to continue. I'll give you some time to think about it and you can give me a call. In the meantime, I'll do what I can."

While Ethan was talking to Harold, Harold's brother-in-law, John, was talking to George. "George, you and I have talked many times about your having a drinking problem." George opened his mouth to say something but John held up his hand, palm out, and said, "Before you say anything, let me tell you that discussions like this are no easier for me than they are for you. You have to remember that when you hit your wife, as you did last night, it's natural for her to call your sister. Then, Joyce feels obligated to help and leans on me to talk to you. And here we are." George's bloodshot downcast eyes seemed glued upon his hands, which he was nervously twisting in his lap. "I know you don't want to admit it, but you do have a drinking problem, George, and until you do admit it, and get some kind of help, it will keep getting worse. The only other thing I have to say is, I hope we don't have to have this conversation again."

George said, "I didn't mean to hit her. I didn't even know that I did"

"You didn't hurt her, thank God, but who knows, next time...."

George put his elbows on the desk and buried his face in his hands. He sat there for a while. Both remained quiet. Then John left.

* * *

George was always sorry after one of his binges, especially after John lectured him. He resented John for it, but knew he was right. He decided, on the spot, it was time to clean up his act. He had done many things because of the drinking and he knew what the first thing was that he had to fix immediately. He raised his head and reached for the telephone.

"Mr. Secontini, This is George Farnsworth. I want to cancel the contract we made."

"You know you don't get the five thousand back."

"I know, and I don't care."

"I'll take care of it," Secontini said, disconnecting their call and immediately dialing another number. "Kavichi, this is Secontini. The Stone contract is cancelled."

"Shit," he said "do I get paid for the work I've put into it already?"

"Don't get you're bowels in an uproar," Secontini said. "You'll get paid."

Kavichi punched the end button on his cell phone, and laying it on the seat of his blue Ford sedan, picked up the earphones and continued to listen. He had put Ethan's office under stakeout and placed a small transmitter in his telephone as soon as Secontini had given him the job. Now, while parked in a parking lot across from Ethan's office, he thought about what a boring job it had been because Williams was hardly ever there. I've put a lot of time and effort into this thing and I'll be damned if I'm just going to give up. This dame's worth a lot of money and if I can grab her, I should be able to get plenty from the family for her release, he reasoned.

* * *

After hanging up from talking with Secontini, George sat back in his chair. It's time to follow through on John's advice and do something about my problem, he thought. I don't want to remain between what I used to be and what I'm becoming. I need to choose one path or the other. John was right. If I don't do something, it'll only get worse. Besides, I'm afraid I might kill myself or someone else. I haven't told Linda yet, but on the way home last night, I almost hit another car, and in swerving to miss it, I nearly hit a pedestrian on the sidewalk. While I managed to miss the woman, I caught a telephone pole with the back fender and right end of the back bumper. As if we don't have enough debt, we'll now have to pay out five hundred dollars deductible to fix the car, and our insurance premium will probably go up.

He found out where local AA meetings were held and forced himself to attend one. It was his turn to stand up and admit his alcoholism to the group. It was not going to be easy, he thought, as he stood up, but if the others can do it, so can I.

"My name is George, and I'm an alcoholic." The group, in unison, welcomed him by his first name. He started his narrative with the events of the previous Friday leading up to and including his fight with Linda, and his internal urge to get away, which caused him to hit her. Feeling drained, he sat down.

Five other people stood and bared their intimate and shameful behavior to the group. Three admitted to alcohol abuse like George and two to drug abuse. They admitted to sexual and physical abuse of their children, involvement in DWIs, hit and run accidents, causing fights in bars, and other less significant acts, some even less severe than George's. All in all, though, the admissions served to strengthen George's resolve to do something about his problem. Following the meeting, there were refreshments of cookies and coffee. While George was eating a cookie and deep in thought about the despicable stories he had just heard, he felt a tap on his shoulder. He turned around and faced a man of about fifty with graying hair that was receding at the part on the right side. He probably had a matching hairline on the other side that was covered by his hair that was combed across and back in a very neat fashion. He extended his hand and said, "I'm James and I've been assigned as your sponsor.

George shook his hand, and he said, "In case you don't know the purpose of a sponsor, it means I'm available day or night if you want someone to talk to. If you feel like you want a drink or need one, don't hesitate to give me a call and we'll talk. It's amazing how much it can help. Even if you just feel down and want to talk to someone, give me a call. Believe me, I know, I've been there. I've been sober for five years and very proud of it. Now I want to help someone else." They talked for a long time and James told George not to beat himself up too much. Instead, move forward with his eye on a new future. They exchanged phone numbers and parted as newfound friends.

When he arrived home, Linda was in bed. He sat down on the bed beside her and gently shook her shoulder. She opened her eyes and was startled for a moment. When she realized it was George and that he was sober, she sat up, wrapped her arms around his neck, and started to cry.

He said, "Don't cry. I'm going to change starting tonight. I'm going to continue to go to the AA meetings. I was assigned a sponsor tonight whom I can call any time, day or night. Linda, I know I've apologized before and made promises before, but thanks to John, I am dead serious this time." Holding her close, he told her how much he loved her and that he was going to make up for all the anxious times he had caused her. He lay down beside her and, holding each other, they fell asleep.

Harold was in the office of his little bookstore working on the computer when the phone rang. When he picked up the receiver, it was George. "Now, George, don't start."

"No, I want to apologize," he said

"That's unique, what's come over you?"

"I've taken the pledge, Harold."

"Yeah, Right."

"I'm serious. I went to my first AA meeting last night and I swear I'm going to stop drinking."

"That's great, George, but one meeting doesn't hack it. You've got a long way to go before I'll believe you've quit. It would be wonderful, though, if you did. I accept your apology and wish you the best of luck with your battle against drinking. If I can help, let me know."

In Baltimore, Ethan was still in his pajamas, drinking a cup of coffee having just finished listening to the news. He had talked to Jeff Johnson and several of his staff members concerning the whereabouts of Sara without success. He decided it was time to give up the search, and he opened his cell phone to call Harold when it rang. The caller ID indicated it was Dr. Lee. "Good morning, Dr. Lee." Ethan almost dropped the phone. "You can't be serious; she's been doing so well! I'll be there as soon as I can." He dressed as fast as possible, raced to the car, tore out of the parking lot, and headed for the hospital.

When he arrived at Beth's room, he was shocked at the sight compared to what he had seen twenty-four hours earlier. She was back on a ventilator and had the intravenous tube back in place. She was very pale and still. The day before, she had smiled, moved her head and hands, and made some utterances.

"Nurse, I have to talk to Dr. Lee immediately!"

"Yes, Mr. Williams. I know he's in the hospital. I'll page him and have him meet you in the waiting room."

Ethan paced the floor while waiting for the doctor. He was alternately pushing the fingers on his hands like he was trying to crack his knuckles but there was no sound. "What happened?" he asked the empty room. Yesterday, he thought, she was getting well, and now she's headed in the opposite direction. I can't stand it. I'll die if she doesn't make it. Tears formed in his eyes. He got tired of pacing after a while, and as he started to sit, the doctor entered the room.

"Dr. Lee, what the hell's going on? Yesterday, Beth was on her way to recovery, and now she appears to be back where she was several weeks ago." Ethan's voice cracked and his eyes started to overflow.

"Ms. Jordon has suffered a setback. The reason is not clear. Perhaps it was the physical therapy, the speech therapy, a combination, or neither. I cannot explain it. It is very clear, however, that there has been some retrogression. I have seen other such cases, and I can give no specific explanation for it."

126

CHAPTER TWENTY-ONE

In his rush to get to the hospital, Ethan had forgotten his cell phone. When he returned to his room, there was a message from Harold waiting for him. Ethan returned the call.

"Harold, it's Ethan."

"Have you made any progress, Ethan? I'm taking all kinds of heat from my brother and sister. I need to tell them something."

"Harold, there's nothing to report."

"With all your personal problems, Ethan, are you doing anything?"

"Things may be going a little slower than normal because of my personal problems, but I'm doing everything I can. Don't forget I've given you the option all along to get someone else, and you've chosen not to. So don't blame me now. It's water over the dam. I've followed every lead I could find to the very end. Some I've gone through more than once taking different paths. So, taking your frustration out on me won't do any good."

"The burdens on me to decide if we should continue or stop the search," Harold said. "I need help."

"I know you want and need results, and you know what? I don't want to let you down; I don't want to quit; and I sure as hell don't want to lose your business. But frankly, Harold, I think it's time to give up. I have no other leads and have no idea of anything else to try. It's up to you, what we do next. I'm certain she's alive, knows I'm looking for her, and has my telephone number. I've been told by a reliable source that she doesn't want to be found. If that's the case, she won't call."

Harold said, "I thought you Investigators had special techniques you used in cases like this."

"This isn't the movies, and I'm only human. I've tried the Maryland DMV, checked the telephone company and the Internet white pages. So she's either left Maryland, doesn't have a car, or is driving a rental. To the rental car point, I've contacted the top ten agencies, and I was stonewalled. Nothing. Since she isn't listed with the telephone company, and doesn't show up on the Internet white pages, she either has an unlisted number, or uses a cell phone. Therefore, I'm stumped. Of course, there's always a chance, and I think there is a probability that she will surface eventually. Then, maybe she'll call."

"All right, Ethan, I'll get back to you, but I don't want to see a bill until this is all over. Thanks for nothing!"

Before he could hang up, Ethan said, "Harold, I'm sorry, but if I should hear something from the feelers I have out, I'll give you a call." They finished the conversation less angry, though no less frustrated, then when it had started.

After Harold talked to Ethan, he asked Joyce and George to come to his house to talk about the Will. He was tired of their constant pressure on him to settle the estate so they could get their hands on the money. He wished his father had picked someone else to be executor.

When the doorbell rang, Becky opened the door and was surprised to see Joyce and George arrive together. Although George had always been civil towards Joyce, he normally would not have picked her up in his car. He always traveled alone. Not having seen him drink lately, Becky realized that this was another example that his attitude toward everyone and everything was certainly improving.

"Come on in," she said. They handed her their coats, and headed for the kitchen. Harold was already seated at the round table in the breakfast area adjacent to the kitchen. "Hi, Joyce, George," he said. "Have a seat." They sat down and Becky offered drinks to lessen the tension that they all had been feeling since the search for Sara started. No one wanted a drink. This was yet another example of the change that had come over George. Normally, he would have had a few before he arrived, and be the first to order when he got there. Now he had shown no signs of drinking for over a week.

Harold spoke first. "I've decided to call off the search for Sara. It's been over two months, and we're no closer to finding her than we were at the beginning." Joyce and

George both smiled and George smacked his hands together and said, "All right! When do we get the inheritance?"

"I just made the decision," Harold said, "and won't know till I talk to Boynton. He controls the next step, which is Probate. I see him day after tomorrow. Probate shouldn't take long, since Sara's the only questionable heir. Other than probate, it's just a matter of Boynton and me completing the financial evaluation. Then the release process will be put into motion."

"Is there anything we can do?" Joyce asked.

"Nope," Harold said, "I have to talk to Boynton."

After Becky served coffee and cake, Joyce and George said their goodbyes and went home.

Charles Boynton's law office was located on the fifth floor of the Federal Building on Clinton Street. Harold arrived about five minutes early for his appointment two days after meeting with Joyce and George. When he entered the office, Boynton was standing at the window looking out over the city. At the sound of the door opening, he swung around and said, "Come on in, Harold, I've been waiting for you. Have a seat." He gestured to a chair in front of his desk.

"Now that you've given up the search, we have to go before the Probate Judge and introduce you as the executor of the will. We'll explain that Sara can't be found, and that you, Joyce, and George, are the only heirs. You'll need to get an affidavit from the private investigator stating what effort he put forth to find Sara, and we'll point out that a public announcement was put in the papers stating that we were looking for her concerning an inheritance.

While we're waiting for the affidavit and an appointment with the judge, we'll complete our evaluation of the estate's worth, and make sure all debts are identified, validated, and paid. You can go through Philip's personal files and papers at home, and in his office, and I'll finish the evaluation of his investment portfolios."

While Harold was meeting with Charles Boynton, Ethan was standing along side Beth's bed watching her. She hadn't moved in a week. The doctor had nothing to offer. He said it was up to Beth, faith and fate. "What the hell does that mean?" Ethan had asked. "In this age of high technology, why can't something be done?" He'd gotten no answers, and his desperation and frustration drained his strength so he cried a lot.

As Ethan was leaving the hospital, he had a call from Harold telling him that the search was off, and he needed an affidavit detailing the search efforts. As depressed as Ethan was, he sure as hell didn't feel like working, but told Harold he'd get it in the mail later in the day or the next.

After his meeting with Boynton, and his call to Ethan, Harold headed for his father's home office. He'd already gone through his father's house and personal effects in his spare time while the search for Sara was going on, and found only a few things of significance. There was a safe that contained his mother and father's marriage license, stock certificates for 800 shares of Wal-Mart stock, 1200 dollars in cash, and some of his mother's jewelry. The contents of the box along with art, antiques, the truck, and the house, were estimated to be worth about two hundred thirty-one thousand dollars.

131

Harold arrived at the house and went straight to his father's office. It was small, neat, and contained only a desk, chairs, a small couch, and two four-drawer file cabinets. He started with the desk. The center and right top drawers contained office supplies. The second drawer down on the right hand side had no divider and contained a stack of Playboy magazines. That's a surprise, Harold thought. The bottom drawer was almost empty. It contained a rag, shoe polish, and a brush for shining shoes. Harold smiled and remembered that his father was always dressed in a suit and his shoes were always shined.

The left top drawer contained a nearly full box of Cuban cigars. He wondered how his father had gotten them. The other drawer on the left side was a file drawer. When he opened it, he was surprised to find only three hanging files, all very thin. One was labeled 'DEBTS OWED', the second 'COLLECTABLE DEBTS', and the third was labeled 'MERRILL LYNCH ACCOUNTS'.

Harold opened the folder marked 'DEBTS OWED'. Inside, there were two sheets of paper. One was a contract for the house that was marked paid in full the previous year. The other was a receipt for his 2004 Silverado pickup marked paid in full two months earlier. So far, it would appear that there were no debts, he thought, as he returned the file to the drawer.

The collectable debts folder was next. It contained more than the first. He was thumbing through it quickly when suddenly, about half way through, something caught his attention, and he stopped. The paper he was looking at was a contract for an interest-free loan in the amount of ten thousand dollars to his brother, George. Nothing had been repaid to-date. He pulled out a pad, made a note, and continued thumbing through the file to the end. He would have to go back to the beginning and check each item in detail, he thought, as he closed the file and laid it on the desk.

The last file held summaries of three accounts. The first summary was for an IRA. It showed a portfolio value as of the end of the previous month of $4,546,328.67. Quite a lot for an IRA, Harold thought, considering that his father, due to his age, would have been making mandatory minimum distributions during the last five years. He made another note on the pad. The second was for a Cash Management Account, which showed a total value of $273,461.42. Harold noted that, closed the file, and returned it to the drawer. In the third summary, there was an Investment account worth $4,572,352.54, which was managed by Merrill Lynch. After making note of that, he put the folder back into the drawer.

In the drawers of the file cabinets, he found catalogs and literature on building materials and suppliers. Apparently, his father had kept well abreast of developments and activities in the building industry.

Sitting down at the desk, he turned his attention back to the 'COLLECTABLE DEBTS' file. There were seven other contracts besides George's in it. They were all interest-free loans and totaled eighty-six thousand dollars including the one to George. Harold and his father got along very well and were very close, but he had no idea his dad was so generous. He would collect the information and present it to Charles Boynton. Charles should be able to explain why his father had been such a benefactor.

CHAPTER TWENTY-TWO

Ethan had just finished his report for Harold, explaining what he had done to find Sara, and how he had failed. After having the document notarized, he put it in the overnight mail and headed for the hospital.

When he entered Beth's room, he stopped short and stared. Her eyes were closed. She was pale, and had more than the usual tangle of tubes around her. For the first time, he had a feeling that she might not recover. He hadn't stopped at the nurse's station on the way in, but now went back to see if there had been any change in her condition.

"I'm sorry, Mr. Williams, she's still non-responsive. We take her vital signs, bathe her, and turn her periodically, but we've seen no change. The doctor has run some tests, but you'll have to talk to him about the results."

"Would you tell him I'll be in Beth's room?"

Ethan was startled out of his thoughts of concern for Beth by the sound of Dr. Lee entering the room, and stood.

"Please, sit, Mr. Williams." As Ethan sat down again, Dr. Lee seated himself on the front edge of the chair next to him. "I would like to talk to you about Ms. Jordon's condition. I believe the nurse told you that we ran some tests."

"Yes."

"We performed an electroencephalogram which gives us a tracing of the variations in electric force in the brain. The graph was flat, meaning there is no brain function. I'm very, very sorry, Mr. Williams, but I must tell you that Ms. Jordon is brain dead."

Before he could say more, Ethan burst into hopeless sobbing. After a moment, "But I was just in there, and she's breathing."

"I'm sorry, but that is the machine breathing for her."

Ethan covered his face with his hands for a moment and then said in a sobbing voice, "She came out of it before, isn't it possible . . ."

"No." Dr. Lee interrupted. The tests before, showed some brain activity, this time there is none. I'm very sorry, and wish I could be more encouraging, but I'm afraid there is no hope."

Continuing to sob and in a daze, Ethan asked, "What do we do, Doctor?"

"Ms. Jordon listed her mother as next of kin. In checking, we find she is in a nursing home and not competent. Further, since she was in under emergency conditions, we have no Living Will on file. And for some reason that no one can explain, her doctor has none either. Do you know if she had one, or what her wishes were?"

"No, but I'll see what I can find out," Ethan said in a dejected tone.

He sat by Beth's bed for a long time thinking. He, and Beth both had dangerous jobs. His was even more dangerous before he had quit and become a PI. Why couldn't he have been killed instead of Beth?

He remembered working for the Syracuse police department when a homicide detective-lieutenant, Jon Broder, requested help from the vice squad. He had a suspect in the Roger Moreland murder case that he wanted a vice detective to help him pursue. Ethan had just come off a case and was given the assignment. When they met, Broder said he thought the suspect, Backus Gibbs, had fled to Baltimore where his mother lived. Ethan told Broader that he knew a detective in the Baltimore Police Department, and he'd be glad to go there. So Ethan called Beth, and she got approval from her lieutenant, Chuck Jones, to support him on the case. He remembered coming to Baltimore and staying in the same motel he was staying in now.

As he entered the motel lobby on that first trip, he saw Beth sitting in a chair facing the reception desk. She appeared even more beautiful then he had remembered her two years earlier when they had split up. Her red curly hair was still long the way he liked it and she was as shapely as he remembered. Approaching her he had said, "We should meet like this more often." She stood and greeted him with a smile and open arms. They hugged and kissed lightly. "Ready?" she had asked. Then they went to police headquarters where he met Chuck Jones. He remembered that day like it was yesterday.

That night, they staked out Backus Gibbs' mother's house. They assumed that Gibbs would show up there eventually, and decided to work in six-hour shifts to provide coverage around the clock. Beth took the first shift since Ethan had just driven down from Syracuse. As unromantic as the arrangement may sound, it provided a good opportunity to start to mend the relationship that had fallen apart two years earlier. They were able to overlap their shifts, have meals in the car together; such as they were, consisting of coffee, donuts, snacks, and sandwiches. As days went by, they were even able to steal a few intimate moments.

The stake out ended at three a.m., less than a week later, with the arrest of Gibbs. They took him back to Syracuse together. During interrogation there, he confessed and identified the individual who had hired him. Beth stayed on in Syracuse to help run down the second suspect. Ethan and she continued to work together and had more after-hours personal time then they had had in Baltimore. Their estranged relationship of two years earlier healed quickly, and they were planning to get married. Ironically, that job which was responsible for their getting back together, was also largely responsible for her being promoted, which in turn, led to the accident that caused her death.

The next day, after Ethan had cried himself out, he called Chuck Jones.

"Chuck, this Is Ethan. I got some horrible news last night."

Before Chuck had a chance to respond, Ethan hurried on nervously, fighting back the tears. "They've got Beth on a ventilator to keep her breathing, but the doctor says she's brain dead."

"My God, Ethan, I'm so sorry! The last time I saw her she was in a coma but doing okay."

"I know." Between sobs, he said, "Dr. Lee says Beth has marked her driver's license to donate her organs. Therefore, he needs to know if she has a Living Will, and I don't know, do you?"

"No, I don't."

"I just picked up her personal things from the hospital and I'm going to look through her apartment. I need to find out about her mother, too. I'll call you later." He hung up and left for Beth's apartment.

The apartment was in a ten story brick building on the north side of Chesapeake Bay a short distance east of Inner Harbor. Ethan parked across the street and approached the building. The door attendant recognized him and said, "Hello, Mr. Williams, how's our favorite girl today?"

"Beth passed away last night, Bert."

"Oh, Dear Mother of God," he said, putting his hand over his mouth. Ethan explained how she had died, and that she hadn't suffered. "Thank God for that." Bert crossed himself.

Ethan took the elevator up to the apartment where he and Beth had made love so many times. It took his breath away getting past the memories brought back by the sight of the bed. As hard as it would be he knew he had to go through the chest, dresser, two nightstands, and closet. He was looking for a Will, a Living Will, and information about Beth's mother, and cemetery plots.

He started with the nightstands. Nothing. Next, he tried the dresser, which contained only clothes. Touching her panties and nightgowns, and smelling her perfume brought back wonderful memories that made him terribly sad. He moved along as quickly as possible.

The four drawers of the chest contained a couple of jewelry boxes, some photo albums, and bedding. He deliberately didn't open the jewelry boxes or photo albums because he knew he couldn't stand it. He thought he'd come back later and go through them.

When Ethan opened the closet and saw more clothes, he broke down and cried. He had to stop and go into the living room to sit down and regain his composure. After a while, he stopped crying and felt able to go back to the closet. On the shelf, there were shoeboxes and two police hats. The hats brought a feeling of elation as he thought about himself and Beth working together, and a feeling of devastation about Beth's death on the job.

On the floor of the closet were more shoeboxes and a gray metal box near the rear left corner. He pulled the box out. It was a heavy, fireproof home safe which looked similar to those he had seen back in Syracuse. He then pulled out Beth's keys and found the one that fit the lock and after getting the safe open he found what he was looking for. She did have a Living Will, which said, 'Do Not Resuscitate'. Reading the words caused tears to flood his eyes again, but after he wiped his already red eyes, and his vision cleared, he continued and came upon a contract that gave the name, address, and telephone number of the nursing home where Beth's mother was living. There was a certificate identifying three burial plots in a cemetery in Syracuse, which were for Beth, her father, and mother. The last thing in the box was Beth's Will, drawn up by a law firm in Syracuse.

CHAPTER TWENTY-THREE

While Ethan was going through Beth's apartment, Sara Stone was starting her new job at Ramax Microelectronics. She went through the door with her name on it into a small reception area containing a desk, three matching file cabinets, two chairs, and a couch. No one was there.

Sara entered her office through the door to the left of the desk, and was as pleased as the first time she saw it. Especially with the bookcase partially filled with operating instructions, company policies, and military specifications. Not only did Ramax have rules and procedures, they were documented and available at her fingertips.

As Sara sat down, there was a soft knock. "Come in," she called out in a strong voice. The door opened, and a middle-aged woman with blond-gray hair and gold-rimmed glasses stepped in.

"Good morning, Susan; come on in."

"Good morning, Ms. Stone. I'm sorry I wasn't at my desk when you arrived, but Mr. Levitt called me away for a few minutes."

Sara smiled. "That's okay, Susan, when the boss calls, we always answer. Are you ready to go to work?"

"Yes, ready and anxious."

"Good, I'd like you to schedule a staff meeting tomorrow at two o'clock."

"Mr. Grady is on a trip and won't be back by then."

"He's Engineering, right?"

"Yes."

"Okay, then schedule it for Friday at two. In the meantime, I'd like you to set up a tickler file. Do you know what a tickler file is?

"Yes, it's a set of file folders numbered one through thirty-one representing each day of the month. Notes can be put into the folders for any future day to remind us of events when the appropriate folder is checked first thing in the morning each day."

"Good, Sara said. After you get the file set up, I'd like you to put a note in it for the third Friday slot reminding us that we'll have a staff meeting every month at the same time. Send a memo to everyone so they'll know to be in town and available on that day.

Now, Susan, there are a couple of things I should tell you.

I'll work late most days but won't expect you to stay past five unless I ask you in advance. You may hold my messages until the end of the day, unless they're urgent, and the first thing each morning, we'll take care of the mail and return telephone calls. Do you have any questions before we get started?"

"Yes. Do you mind personal calls?"

Sara smiled and said, "Not at all, as long as they don't interfere with our business, and I'm sure that won't be a problem, right?"

"Right." She returned Sara's smile. "One other thing, Ms. Stone, how do you take your coffee?"

"I take it with nothing in it, but I won't expect you to get me coffee except when we have visitors. When you get it for them, you may get one for me, too. Otherwise, I'll get my own. I appreciate your asking. Is there anything else?" Sara asked.

"I don't think so," Susan answered.

"Good, now we can officially start working together," Sara said, as she reached across the desk to shake hands with her new secretary.

Susan went back to her desk to do as she was told, thinking about her first meeting with her new boss. She sure seemed nice and wasn't upset that Susan was away from her desk when Sara came in. Of course, Susan was away because of Mr. Levitt, but wouldn't make a habit of doing that, not without good reason, anyway. At least she's someone I can question if I need to know something, Susan thought. Sitting down, she decided the new boss and she were going to get along very well.

Ethan sat on the couch in Beth's apartment and read her will. She had left everything to him, and had named her lawyer, Don Wright, Executor. In naming Ethan her heir, she stipulated that he was to look after her mother's needs, except for the cost of the nursing home, and make sure the nursing home took good care of her. Her mother's money was almost gone, and Beth had decided that her mother would go on Medicaid when it was depleted.

Beth's possessions consisted of her clothes, furniture, car, a 1998 Chevy Lumina, and a bank account containing $6400. When he had gone through the rest of her apartment, he found in the top drawer of the buffet in the dining room, in addition to the bankbook, a key to a safe deposit box, a lease for the apartment, and a title showing that her car was paid for. He wondered why they weren't in the safe with the other important papers, not that it mattered. He would ask the attorney how to proceed, and if he could make funeral arrangements. He picked up the telephone and called Don Wright.

The lawyer told Ethan he would contact the bank and, as Executor of the Will, make sure authority was provided to the bank for him to access the safe deposit box. He told Ethan, under the circumstances, he could check and list the contents of the box and bring that list along with all the other legal information to Syracuse. They would review the material, and then he would process the will. Probate would not be necessary, since the estate was very small and there was only one heir.

Ethan made an appointment to be in Wright's office a week from the coming Friday. That would give him almost two weeks to take care of all the arrangements. He and Beth had discussed death and burial, and both felt that cremation was the most practical approach. Since she had a burial plot back in Syracuse alongside her father, Ethan would take her ashes back with him for burial there. He had decided there would be a Memorial Service in Baltimore with two hours for calling.

"Dr. Lee, here's a copy of Beth's Living Will. Her instruction is 'Do Not Resuscitate'," Ethan said.

"Thank you, Mr. Williams. We will now follow Ms. Jordon's instructions on both life support and organ donation."

"I'd like to say goodbye first," Ethan said.

"Of course, I'll be at the nurse's station. You can let me know when you are finished."

What if I go in and she's awake? He thought. I know that's not possible, but, God, wouldn't it be wonderful if she were. We could kiss, and talk, and plan on what to do when she gets out of here. Tears welled up in his eyes as he snapped out of it and approached her side. He reached into his pocket and pulled out the engagement ring he'd bought and never had a chance to give her. He took her left hand in his, looked at her, and as he slipped the ring on her finger, said, "Beth, I love you so much." He leaned over and kissed her on the lips alongside the tube that was breathing for her, then whispered, "Goodbye, My Darling," and left the room, eyesight blurred, wondering how he would ever fill the hole in his heart.

CHAPTER TWENTY-FOUR

"Ethan was sitting in his hotel room looking out the window at the Chesapeake Bay in the distance. Instead of enjoying the picturesque scene, he was feeling sorry for himself and thinking about Beth's death. Something he could not change. I should concentrate on the job at hand, he kept telling himself, but he couldn't seem to focus no matter how hard he tried. His cell phone rang and brought him out of his misery.

"This is Harold, Ethan, have you found out any more about Sara? I'm ready to go over to Charles Boynton's office to start things rolling on the settlement of the will."

"Nothing," he said in a harsh tone, upset because his thoughts had been interrupted. "I told you I'd call if I had anything."

"Damn, Ethan, you don't have to bite my head off! I haven't heard from you in almost two weeks. What am I supposed to tell my family? You could keep in touch, even if you don't have anything to report. At least I'd know. As it is, I sit here totally in the dark. I think I've been pretty sympathetic and lenient because of your problems. Now you have to start giving some consideration to mine. End of speech, and I'm sorry I bothered you, but I expect you to call soon." He hung up.

"I'll talk to you later, Harold," Ethan said to the dead phone as he returned it to its cradle.

After his unpleasant phone call to Ethan, Harold went to Charles Boynton's office. He and Charles went through their usual pleasantries, and Charles had coffee brought in. Harold told him what he had found in his father's office.

Boynton said, "Let's talk about the 'No Interest Loans'. Your father was a very generous man. Most of those people he gave loans to didn't ask for help. He saw that they were struggling financially, for one reason or another, and found pleasure in trying to help them. Sometimes, he almost forced them to take the help.

Your brother, George, was no exception. At the time, he didn't have a drinking problem and was fresh out of college trying to get his new business started. Being the first-born and the first, and it turned out the only one to graduate from college, your father was anxious to see him succeed. He wanted to give him the money, but the most George would accept was an interest-free loan. When you looked at the records, I'm sure you saw that hardly any of the borrowers repaid their loans. That didn't bother your father. When I would mention it, he'd say, 'Aw, they'll

147

repay it when they can'. And that would be the end of the discussion.

Your dad managed his individual retirement account, and the distributions from that IRA went into his cash management account. The CMA had checking, and he used it for his personal needs. His pension and social security checks were also deposited into the CMA account. A financial analyst helped him manage both.

The money I control is invested in well-diversified portfolios by the trust departments of four different banks. The portfolios are each in a separate Trust, and are now collectively worth just over twenty-three million dollars. I'm the Trustee of each Trust with complete control. My intent is, unless you, as Executor object, to liquidate the Trusts at the appropriate time, so the assets can be available to divide amongst the heirs."

"That's okay with me," Harold responded.

Boynton said, "I can liquidate the Trusts with a few phone calls and arrange for cashier's checks. For the other accounts, we'll have to get some papers to sign. You'll sign as Executor, and I as Philip's official attorney. We should be able to conclude all those activities shortly after we clear probate. You can set up a meeting with your brother and sister on Monday, and we can officially read the Will and set a timetable, if necessary, for concluding any loose ends. I think that's it for now, Harold. They stood, shook hands, and Harold left.

At the same time Harold was leaving Boynton's office in downtown Syracuse, Ethan was leaving the church in Baltimore where the Memorial Service for Beth had just been held. It was a sad experience for him. It seemed so

148

final, which, of course, it was. He planned to pick up Beth's ashes on Thursday and take them back to Syracuse for burial. He had moved out of the motel, moved his things into Beth's apartment, and returned his rental car already. He planned to use Beth's Lumina to return to Syracuse for the burial, and to meet with her attorney. He would leave Thursday right after he picked up her ashes.

A week before the Service, he had met with the funeral director to make the arrangements. The director had gone through his spiel concerning choice of caskets, cost estimates for flowers, choices for a preacher, and costs for facility usage. Ethan sat quietly and courteously until he had finished the list and totaled the numbers, which were astronomical. In keeping with Beth's wishes, Ethan told him that Beth's body would be cremated. Therefore, there would be no preacher or eulogy, no casket, no flowers, and minimal usage of his facilities, because the Service would be small and simple. "Since the body will be cremated I want to rent the casket for showing her body, and I'll purchase a small and simple urn for burial," Ethan said.

"But, Mr. Williams, I'm not sure a rental casket is available."

"Well. Mr. Shropp, if you can't handle it, I'll find someone who can."

"Let me see what I can do. I'm sure I can work out something."

"All right. Here's my cell phone number. I'd like you to call me with a cost and tell me when I can pick up the ashes."

Shropp had called the next day, agreed with Ethan's wishes, given him a reasonable cost, and told him he could pick up the ashes on Thursday.

*   *   *

Ethan's trip to Syracuse went well, though he felt uneasy knowing that Beth's ashes were in the back seat. He went straight to his office and called Don Wright. When his secretary answered, Ethan told her to tell Beth's attorney that he was on his way.

Don was a big man in both height and across the shoulders. His close-cropped sandy hair was un-parted and tapered neatly all round. He had uneven, slightly yellow teeth and gray lifeless eyes. His big nose was casting a shadow over a set of fat lips and protruding chin. A man you could easily pick out in a crowd but one you would not consider very attractive.

"Good morning, Ethan," he said, "Have a seat. You've read Beth's will, so you know she named me Executor. Her estate's not large, and she has no heirs except her mother who's in a nursing home with Alzheimer's. Because of that, Beth left everything to you with the understanding that you would look after her mother's welfare. I won't go over all her possessions in detail since you know what they are. With the key you found and gave me, we'll open the box on Thursday after the burial, and then there is an insurance policy for five thousand that she took out, and one at work for thirty-five thousand. I'd like you to talk to her boss about the latter and ask him to give me a call."

The urn was made of a simulated marble material and shaped like a small chest. The opening of the grave was traumatic for Ethan, and the closing, preceded by a short prayer and placement of the urn, was worse.

*   *   *

The First National Bank was located on Eastern Avenue and sat back from the street landscaped with grass, shrubbery, and two red maple trees in front. The bank was small and not busy. As Ethan and Don Wright approached the counter, the clerk asked, "May I help you?"

"Yes," Wright said. Introducing himself and Ethan, he explained the situation, gave her the key, and signed the card documenting access.

The clerk brought the box out and led them to a small private room. When they opened it, their mouths fell open. It was filled with hundred dollar bills. There were two rows of bills, four stacks in each row. Wright counted one stack. It took a while. He looked at Ethan with eyebrows raised, and said, "400 bills."

Ethan frowned. Making a quick mental calculation, he said, "Holy hell, that's $320,000. Where would she get that kind of money?" He thought, god, that's going to be mine. What will I do with it? To Wright, he said "She never mentioned it to me. What do we do about it?"

"It's an asset," he said, "We'll list it, along with everything else in the estate for tax purposes. For now, we'll leave it in the bank."

Ethan's first stop after returning to Baltimore was police headquarters. As usual, he had to go through the 'who do you want to see?' routine with the desk sergeant before going back to see Chuck Jones. Although Beth no longer officially worked for Chuck at the time just before the accident, Ethan felt Chuck knew her a lot better than her new boss of a few weeks.

"Hey, Ethan, how's it going?"

"Okay, I guess. Chuck, there's a few things I need to talk to you about."

"Shoot."

"First, I wanted to let you know that I buried Beth's ashes. Second, the Executor of her Will asked me to have her boss call him about her life insurance at work. I know you weren't her boss at the time but thought you could take care of it for me. Here's his number.

Lastly, what I want to discuss with you is a little difficult for me since I'm her beneficiary. Her Executor and I opened her safe deposit box and found $320,000 dollars. Do you have any idea where she would get that kind of money?"

"None," Chuck said incredulously.

Ethan's cell phone rang. He turned sideways and said, "Hello."

"Hello, Ethan, This is Don Wright."

"Hi Don, what's up?"

"The money we found in Beth's box has really been bugging me, so I had one of our clerks look into our records. Since our firm did her will, and because of the amount of money we found, I thought someone else in the firm might have worked with her before me. If that was the case, for some reason, she didn't tell me about it. It was a long shot, but I tried it anyway. Talk about the luck of the Irish? I don't know whether you know it or not, but Beth's mother was married twice."

"No, I didn't. I know her father died about ten years ago."

"That's true, and her mother remarried about two years ago and the marriage only lasted about six months."

"She never told me. What happened?"

"It seems that the first inkling that the new husband got that Beth's mother was in the early stages of Alzheimer's, he filed for divorce."

"How do you know all of this?" Ethan asked.

"He was one of our clients, and our firm handled the divorce. He had quite a lot of money, and guess what? There was no prenuptial agreement. So to get out of the marriage at minimal cost he negotiated a quick settlement by giving Natalie Jordon $450,000. She was very upset and, although she wanted to be through with him, she didn't want his money. She had the attorney prepare a document presenting it to Beth as a gift and told the new husband to go to hell."

"Why didn't Beth tell me about this?" Ethan asked of himself more than of Don.

"I don't know," Wright responded, but apparently the $320,000 is what's left. My firm, but not I, was involved with the settlement and the gift document, so most of what I just told you is a matter of our records. The part of the 320k being left from the 450 is conjecture on my part. The nursing home told me their cost is between 20 and 30 thousand a year, and Beth's mother has been private paying for about a year. If you take into consideration the amount allowed as a tax-free gift and the amount of tax on the rest then subtract the nursing home cost for a year, it comes out very close to the $320,000. It all makes sense to me. Incidentally, I informed the nursing home that Beth died, and her mother was not a beneficiary. They said they'd start the paperwork to get her on Medicaid right away."

Ethan thanked Wright for calling and hung up; his mind trying to digest what he had just heard.

CHAPTER TWENTY-FIVE

It was Monday morning. Joyce, George, and Charles Boynton were in Boynton's conference room on the third floor of the Federal Building on Clinton Street waiting for Harold to arrive. Charles was standing with his back to the room, looking out the window at the Syracuse Dome. His mind was not on the business he was about to conduct, because the Syracuse basketball team was going to play the semifinal game of the Big East Final Four. Syracuse had come from twenty-fifth place to the finals. They would play Texas tonight in New Orleans for second place, and the chance to play Kansas for the championship. Charles had a sizeable bet on the Orangemen, and had a big party planned at his house to watch the game.

The door slammed, bringing everyone's attention to Harold's arrival. As he sat down, he said, "I'm sorry I'm late Charles. Go ahead with the reading of Dad's Will.

Charles put a transparency on the old-fashioned overhead projector and said "Harold has asked me to officially read the Will and present the data that we have developed. He also asked me to confirm that he has decided to call off the search for Sara. Therefore, the estate will be divided equally amongst the three of you. They all smiled and looked at Harold. George clapped.

After the reading of the will, Charles switched on the projector. The slide showed columns of numbers detailing the assets of the estate and where they came from. No one but Harold paid any attention to the detail. The others were only interested in the figure at the bottom that showed the amount to be inherited. That number was just over nine million dollars for each of them. Joyce and George were surprised. From what they had heard from Charles and Harold in the beginning, they expected no more then six million each. George slapped his leg; Joyce turned toward George and smiled. She said, "Wow, all right!" Harold didn't smile. He still felt guilty about giving up the search and asked, "Don't you guys feel anything about giving up the search for our sister?"

"Yeah, richer," George replied. "Why the hell have you taken so long to call off the search? We should have been moving faster."

"That's right," Joyce added, "with Sara out of the picture, we each get a third instead of a fourth, and we ought to be moving along faster, still"

Harold, disgusted with his brother and sister, motioned for Charles to turn off the projector.

George was the most elated. He was thinking how he would pay off his debts and invest part of the money to back up the business. The first debt he would pay off would be the ten thousand dollars he had borrowed from his dad to pay his gambling debt. Philip had seen George struggling with his newly started business, and insisted that he allow him to help. Finally, George gave in with the understanding that it was a loan and not a gift. Philip agreed, but at the same time, insisted that it be a loan at no interest. He never knew that the money went to pay a gambling debt rather than to help the business.

George knew that equal shares of the money should be given to Harold, Joyce, and himself when he repaid the loan. He would tell Charles, though, to divide it equally between Joyce and Harold and use his own judgment as to the explanation. Next, he would pay off the hi-interest credit cards. After that, he would pay off the house, car, and boat in that order. Then he would be a debt-free man, and now that he wasn't drinking anymore, he should be able to keep his life under control. There were two other things he thought he'd do. He would invest some money, the interest of which would be specifically for Linda to spend as she pleased. He would then invest what was left, and use the income from that for vacations and other things they wanted. The principal, he would leave for retirement.

Joyce could envision the expansion of their business. Of course, that decision would be John's. There were a number of things she would like to have: a new house, a new car, a new wardrobe and travel to lots of places that she had dreamed about for a long time.

Harold and Becky had talked about what they would do with the money for some time. They would move the business into a larger shop near the present one in the same shopping center. That way they would be able to maintain their location identity and customers. They would also open a second store in a nearby newer and larger mall. They would build a new house that would have a room for the baby that they could now afford to have.

Charles concluded the meeting by saying, "You know, people, there's something you should think about. What if Sara shows up? I requested a probate court date when your father died. That was almost four months ago. We could conceivably get a date at any time and clear probate immediately, or it might take a lot longer. There's no way of knowing. If she should show up before probate, the Will is quite clear. If it's after probate, I don't know. Then it'll be up to the court. If I were you, I wouldn't spend all of the money just yet. Anyway, if everything continues to move along smoothly, I'll transfer the funds to your respective banks as soon as the Will gets through probate.

When he was alone, Boynton sat down and thought about the Farnsworth inheritance. He was used to handling the Farnsworth money and so was the firm. Neither one wanted to lose the account now. He leaned across the desk, pulled a legal pad into place, and started to work on a strategy to bring most of the money back into the fold of the firm.

At the kitchen table of the modest rancher on River Road, Harold and Becky sat drinking a cup of coffee. "Becky, we've known about the inheritance for a good

157

while, but now that we actually have it, or will have it in a few months, what are we going to do? We're millionaires! It's not possible to spend that kind of money."

"Oh, Harold, honey, let's not worry about it. We'll do the things we talked about first. That will probably take one day's interest from the money." She smiled and Harold laughed.

"It probably won't even take that," he said. "The things we talked about can probably be paid for with the executor's fee." He reached across the table, took her hand and said, "Let's go make that baby. It's free."

George stood in front of the desk of Charles Boynton's secretary, waiting for her to get off the phone. "I have an appointment with him in five minutes," he said.

"You may go in; he's expecting you."

"Good morning, George. What can I do for you?"

"Before I tell you why I'm here, I want to ask you to work as fast as you can to get us the inheritance funds. Before I leave today, I'll make an appointment to come back and discuss ways in which you might help me manage mine.

I know when you and Harold went through my father's things, you must have found a record of a loan he made to me. I intended all these years to pay it back, but for one reason and another, I didn't. Now, I can and will. I want it to come out of my share of the estate and divided between Joyce and Harold. I don't want any of it to come back to me."

"I can make that happen, George, but you are entitled to your share."

"I know, but the way I've been in the past — the drinking, the way I treated my father, the way I treated my brother and sister — let's say it's a small gesture of self-retribution."

"Very well, George, I'll take care of it."

CHAPTER TWENTY-SIX

It was one o'clock when Sara had finished her first staff meeting and had lunch. The meeting went much smoother than she expected. The managers in place when she took the job were as qualified and impressive in person as they were on paper.

With her office organized and beginning to feel at home, calling Mark Hefron was next on her agenda. She picked up the telephone and dialed his number.

"Mark, this is Sara."

"Sara! It's great to hear your voice. Where are you?"

"I'm in Rochester, Irondequoit, actually. I wanted to let you know I've taken a job with Ramax Microelectronics and I want to give you my new telephone number."

"Great." He reached for a pen.

As soon as she gave him the number, she added, "I would still like you to check with me before giving it to anyone else."

"Sure, Sara, no problem."

"Oh, and while we're talking about telephone numbers, Would you give me the number of the private investigator who asked about me. Now that I have things under control again, I thought I might give him a call."

Mark gave her the number and she asked, "How have things been going with you and TTT since I left?"

"Oh, about the same. You know. Jeff keeps screwing up, blaming the rest of us, and then giving us hell for not fixing the problems fast enough."

"Mark, we've discussed this before. You can't let him put you down. You really have to stand toe-to-toe with him and give it right back."

"I know." Changing the subject, he said, "Hey, how about going sailing Sunday?"

"I'd love to. I'll fly down Saturday and meet you at the boat around ten. Will that work?"

"Works great for me. Works even better sooner, if you'd like."

"No. We'll make it Saturday. See you then, Mark. Bye."

They hung up and Sara turned to her computer. She had a lot of work to do if she was going to get away for the weekend.

Sara was having a hard time deciding what to pack. The weather was turning nice. The reports were for temperatures to be in the high 60's to low 70's over the weekend with cloudless, sunny skies. Definitely not

161

swimming weather, but then it might be warm enough to lie in the sun, so she put in a bathing suit. She also put in slacks and a sweater to wear while sailing, and a windbreaker just in case it was cooler than predicted. Ready and packed, she headed for the airport.

The marina hadn't changed since the last time Sara had been there. The 'Sunset Pleasure' was in her slip halfway down the dock. As Sara walked towards the boat, she saw Mark come out of the hatch. She picked up her pace, waved, and called out to him. Giving her a big smile, he waved back. Along side the boat, she said, "Permission to come aboard, Captain?"

"If you're the new first mate, permission granted."

"And if I'm not?"

"Permission granted anyway."

She climbed aboard, and they embraced fervently and kissed in a manner showing more than casual friendship. Mark held her at arm's length. "Sara, I've really missed you."

"I've missed you, too, Mark." They kissed again, longer and more passionately.

Sara sucked in her breath and said, "Whew, give a girl some air." He laughed and squeezed her harder.

Mark pulled his head back and looked at her as she stood there squinting against the sun shining in her face. He was, and had always been, taken with her beauty. He released his hold on her, took her right hand in his left, brushed her small turned up nose with the end of his index finger and, gesturing at the mast, said, "I thought we'd sail out a short distance and just drift while we have brunch."

"Wow, he cooks, too." She smiled.

"At least the first or second best chef on the boat. You man the lines, Mate, and I'll start the iron sail."

Away from the dock and out far enough to maneuver, Sara brought the 'Sunset Pleasure' into the wind, and Mark raised the mainsail. He wouldn't bother with the jib until after they were finished eating, and had begun their longer sail.

Sara held the boat steady into the wind keeping the sail fluttering in the breeze while Mark came to the stern to take the wheel. Sara moved aside and yielded control to him as he steered the boat across the wind, and cut the engine. They were under sail. Sara moved over and sat beside him.

They sailed into the rising sun enjoying the quietness of the hull cutting through the relatively calm water, and watched the sunlight dance off the small ripples. Before long, Mark said, "Hungary?"

"Starved."

He brought the boat into the wind and asked Sara to take the wheel while he lowered the sail. After they had stowed the sail on the boom, Mark went forward to drop the anchor. The wind had picked up a little, and he thought it unwise to let the boat drift while they ate.

"Come on, the galley chef will need a little help," he said. They went below to fix fruit, bagels and coffee.

They brought the food to the cockpit where Mark had a small folding table stowed below one of the side bench seats. He set it up while Sara held the tray containing the food. They sat across from each other and ate quietly for a few minutes before Mark asked, "Did you contact the PI who was asking about you?"

"No, I plan to do that as soon as I get back. Mark, you make a mean fruit salad and bagel." She chuckled.

"What can I say, my mother told me the way to a girl's heart is through her stomach."

"She had that right," Sara said, as she took a spoonful of fruit followed by a bite of bagel.

"Where would you like to sail to?" Mark asked.

"I don't know, make a suggestion."

"How about Evergreen Park? We could make it by lunch time."

"Just like a man. Not even through breakfast, and already thinking about lunch. That sounds fine. We can eat at that little hotdog stand."

"That's what I had in mind, knowing what a cheap date you are."

She continued the good-natured banter by saying, "I fly all the way down here from Rochester and you take me out for a hotdog."

"Sara, now that I know you work in Rochester, and I know your phone number, I have to ask why you have been so secretive about your move."

She turned toward him with a sorrowful look in her eyes and was quiet for a moment. Then she spoke. "Before we became friends, in fact, before I hardly knew you, I spent a night in a hotel with Jeff.

"Sara, you don't have to explain."

"No, Mark, I want to. She proceeded to tell him in detail what happened and then said, "I am very ashamed of that night and was reluctant to tell you for fear that it might hurt our relationship.

"Sara, nothing could hurt our relationship. If anything, it will strengthen it."

"You're wonderful," she said and kissed him. "I hated not telling you when I made the move, but the time just didn't seem right. I was secretive because I was afraid if Jeff knew where I was before I was settled in a new job he might use it as leverage to try and force me to come back. Even worse, I was afraid he might use it as a way of preventing me from getting a better job. Now that I'm settled into my new position, I don't care about my past indiscretions. I asked you to keep things quiet a little longer, however, because I don't want Jeff bothering me about problems at TTT."

He could see that her eyes were watery, so he took her in his arms and held her.

CHAPTER TWENTY-SEVEN

Their naked bodies were covered with a thin layer of sweat. It was cool outside but hot in the cabin. They had just finished making love. "Darling, I don't know if I can stand us being so far apart," Sara said.

"It's not that bad," Mark replied. "It's less than a day's drive between Rochester and Baltimore, and only an hour by air. Since we both feel we're not interested in marriage or children, at least for now, we can have the best of both worlds.

We can keep our jobs and spend weekends together, one weekend at my place, one at your place, then one here on the boat. Other than that, we can have private weekends for ourselves, or go on trips and take vacation time for longer getaway trips. How does that sound?"

"Wonderful," she said, as she rolled over and kissed him. They lay in each other's arms until they fell asleep.

It was about eleven when they awoke. Sara made coffee and they drank it while sitting on the bow. They decided there was still time to reach Evergreen Park for their hotdog and get back before dark. Mark started the engine, pulled the anchor, and hoisted the mainsail while Sara held the wheel. Then, he took the wheel while she put up the jib. Then she came aft and collapsed in the seat alongside him. Puffing, she said, "You'll have to hire another mate."

"Why?"

"Two reasons. First, I can't hack it. Second, I'd rather be here." She kissed him on the cheek and snuggled up against his chest.

Sara awoke as Mark was approaching the dock at Evergreen Park. "I'll do the lines." She yawned, stood up and reached back to grab the stern line. The hot dog stand where they were having dinner wasn't much more than a shack. It was known, however, to have the best hotdogs around. They advertised dogs with sauerkraut, chili, cheese, hot or mild salsa, and of course, onions, relish, catsup and three kinds of mustard.

On the way back, they lashed the wheel down, sat close, and had dessert and made love.

In her office Monday morning, Sara had made a list of things to do for the day and was reaching for the telephone to call Ethan when it rang.

"Hi, Sara. It's Bert. Have you seen this morning's Wall Street Journal?" The paper was spread out in front of him on the desk.

"No, I was out of town for the weekend and came into the office early to play catch-up. Normally, the first thing I do is look at the paper, but this morning, I've been preoccupied with what I need to do. What did I miss?"

"Big headline. 'CHILD CHOKES TO DEATH ON PART FROM TTT TOY TRAIN'"

"Oh my God," Sara said, leaning back in her chair.

This may sound cold, Levitt said, but after your interview, Sara, I sold my Teeter stock. It looks like that was a smart move. Did this problem have something to do with you leaving TTT?"

"Not directly, but related. Jeff's overall business approach, which I described to you during the interview, played a big part in the problem that caused that accident. I'm glad I left when I did."

Sara called Mark. "Good morning, Mark, I haven't seen the morning's Journal yet, but my boss told me about the child dying from choking on the train part."

"The lawyers have already filed a lawsuit," Mark said, in a despondent tone, and the amount is one hundred million. I'm due in a meeting with our attorneys in five minutes, so I have to go."

"I won't keep you, Mark. Call me if I can be of help." Sara hung up and sat thinking. She didn't want to see Mark get caught in the quagmire created by Jeff Johnson. She was being very careful not to let Johnson get her involved in TTT problems again. However, she would help Mark if he needed it, regardless of cost or Johnson.

After a while, Sara picked up the telephone and placed her call to the private investigator. "May I speak to Ethan Williams, please?"

"This is Williams."

He sounded much younger than she expected. Her perception of PIs was heavy set, white-haired guys with gruff voices. "This is Sara Stone. I understand you've been trying to contact me."

Holy shit, Ethan thought, coming out of his chair and his hand flying to his forehead like he had a sudden headache. Here she is, out of the blue. I only hope she's not too late. "Yes, I have, Ms. Stone. I need to talk to you about an inheritance."

"An inheritance!" Sara exclaimed.

"Yes, your biological father, Philip Farnsworth, has named you, along with your two half brothers and half sister in his Will. It's important that all parties involved get together right away to go over the details. Where are you located?"

"Oh!" she said, "I've got two brothers and a sister?" Her eyes watered, and she said, "What are their names?"

"Harold, George, and Joyce," Ethan replied.

She thought, how could my mother let me go all those years and not tell me? And why didn't they try to contact me earlier? Were they that ashamed? Did my brothers and sister even know, or were they in the dark all these years like me? Sara covered the mouthpiece of the phone, sniffed and wiped her eyes. How could my mother hurt me so much in order to spite my father. I know we didn't get along very well, but she just didn't seem that mean. Sara sniffed again, wiped her eyes, composed herself and taking an aggressive attitude to hide her emotions, removed her hand from the mouthpiece, and said, "Mr. Williams, how do I know you are who you say you are?"

"My Private Investigator's License is on record with the State of New York and my company, 'ETHAN WILLIAMS INVESTIGATIONS' is registered here in Onondaga County. You can check those out. Also you can call the attorney for the Farnsworth estate, Charles Boynton, and he will verify what I just told you. So you know it's legitimate, you can get his telephone number from the phone company. He works for the firm of Shepard, Shane, and Barnes here in Syracuse.

"Okay, Sara responded, I'll Check. I'm in Rochester."

"Good, Ethan said, I'm in Syracuse. It would be best and fastest if you could come here since the Executor, your brothers, your sister and the estate attorney are also here."

"I can come there," she said. "When?"

"Time is critical, Ethan said, how about today or tomorrow, since we are so close?"

Looking at her schedule and estimating the driving time, she said, "I can be there at three this afternoon,"

"Great, my office is in Baldwinsville." He gave her directions and started to hang up when she said, Mr. Williams, I have a Mercedes company car, and it has a broken taillight. I have a 12:00 appointment at the dealer to have it fixed. I plan to have lunch while they do the work so it shouldn't interfere with our meeting. I just wanted you to know in case I'm a little late. Ethan thanked her for the information and hung up.

Kavichi was sitting in his car across from the PI's office. In his earphones, he heard the ringing from the bug he had put in the phone, and then a woman's voice; "May I speak to Ethan Williams, please?"

"This is Williams."

"This is Sara Stone. I understand you've been trying to contact me."…

After listening to the complete conversation between Ethan and Sara, Kavichi left the earphones on and smiling, sat thinking, the time is near. He didn't wait long for the next call.

"Harold, it's Ethan, I've found Sara."

"That's great," he said, thinking frantically about the Will and the inheritance dilemma it presented for him as Executor. "I mean from the standpoint of finding our sister. From the standpoint of the Will, I think it presents some serious problems. Where is she?"

"She's in Rochester, but she'll be here in my office this afternoon at three. Can you be here then?"

"Yeah, no problem. I'll invite my brother and sister and Charles Boynton, too, if you can handle that many at one time in your office."

"See you then," Ethan said, hanging up, and crossing the office to make a pot of coffee.

171

CHAPTER TWENTY-EIGHT

The board members were taking a break and having coffee. They were standing around in groups of two and three talking. The Directors of Teeter Tot Toys were holding their usual quarterly meeting, which was called back to order by the chairman, Jeff Johnson. Everyone filled their coffee cups and took their seats. The meeting had been in session for about two hours and all the old business on the agenda had been taken care of. Johnson now asked, "Is there any new business to bring before the Board?"

Conrad Enders, a man in his late fifties with a full head of white hair, a white mustache and brown eyebrows raised his hand.

"Enders?"

"Mr. Chairman, I make a motion that we vote on the removal of Jeff Johnson from his position as President and CEO, of Teeter Tot Toys."

Johnson had been expecting this. The latest fiasco with the train set was about to bring him down. He had been lobbying the board members for two and a half months since the lawsuit had been initiated. He thought he was doing pretty well and gaining enough support to survive the problem. But now he wasn't sure since they had just lost the lawsuit for one hundred million dollars. Today would tell the tale.

"I second the motion," said Fester Palmer, the obese man at the side of the table on Johnson's right with an unlit cigar in his mouth.

"I think we should give Jeff a chance to defend himself," said the round-faced, balding man, Sherwood Henson, sitting next to Johnson.

"Questions on the motion," said Keefer Black, the skinny man sitting at the opposite end of the table from the chairman. Black was at one time a supporter of Johnson but now questioned Johnson's leadership ability. Johnson had promised him a substantial raise in salary and a new car as a board member in exchange for his support. When Black told him he couldn't be bought, Johnson knew he had taken the wrong approach with him.

On a seven-man board, Johnson only needed three supporters in addition to himself. He knew he could count on Henson and Flowers and he knew he had lost Black and was on shaky ground with the other three. With the lobbying he had done, he was hoping that at least one of them would end up voting in his favor.

"I'm still not sure we should act so hastily," said Bess Flowers. She was a plump woman in her early fifties that had been sleeping with Johnson for over a year and a half. He maintained her condo in Timonium and she was afraid if he were voted out she might lose her position on the board as well as her condo. She was squirming in her seat and her voice was somewhat garbled from the earpiece of her gold-rimmed glasses, which she had in her mouth.

"What the hell do you mean 'hastily', Bess?" the obese man across the table with the unlit cigar responded. "We just lost the goddamn 100 million dollar law suit because of his incompetence and the frigging stock is down fifty percent. What do you want to wait for, bankruptcy?"

Johnson didn't like the tone of Fester Palmer's voice. It didn't sound like there was much chance for his support. Johnson said, "Look! This is the third time we've discussed this matter and I want to remind you again that the company has done pretty well under my leadership. At the same time, it *is* unfortunate that the train-part accident occurred on my watch and the damn jury decision went against us in the lawsuit. I still maintain, however, that that problem was no fault of mine. The vender's material was defective," Johnson continued, as perspiration started to bead up on his forehead, "and we *were* in the process of doing a recall when the accident occurred. Besides, we will appeal the decision."

"Sure; we'll appeal," Enders said, "but you don't understand, Jeff. The accident should never have happened."

Ben Branch spoke up next, his ebony skin shining in the glancing light from the window. "You know, Jeff, you say it was the vendor's fault, but I remember the lead problem with the game pieces and the acid problem with the play money. If it hadn't been for us directing you to hire Sara Stone who bailed us out of those problems, it's hard to tell where we would be at this point. Now, you've caused her to leave the company which, in my opinion, is another example of your inadequate leadership ability. As Vice Chairman, I'm calling for a vote. All in favor of removing Jeff Johnson as President and Chief Executive Officer of Teeter Tot Toys at the end of this month raise your hand." Four hands went up. "Now, all those opposed." Sherwood Henson, Bess Flowers, and Jeff Johnson raised their hands. ·

Johnson's face turned white; his jaw dropped, and he sat down. Turning towards the secretary, the Vice Chairman said, "Let the record show that the vote was four to three in favor of removing Jeff Johnson from his position as President and CEO of Teeter Tot Toys effective as of the end of the current month. Also, let the minutes show that he is no longer chairman or a member of the board and that there will be a special board meeting next Wednesday to take up the subject of a replacement for Johnson. This meeting is adjourned."

CHAPTER TWENTY-NINE

Mark had been sitting in his office at the end of the week after hearing the court ruling on the wrongful death suit of the child that had choked to death on the TTT train part. He was devastated by both the child's death and, as Vice President of Finance for the company, the resulting lawsuit. His biggest fear was that, under Jeff Johnson's management, the same thing could and probably would happen again. His next fear was how the company would be able to survive the financial burden. Then Ben Branch came into his office and said, "Do you have a few minutes, Mark?"

"Sure, Ben, what can I do for you?"

"As you probably know, Mark, we had our quarterly Board meeting Wednesday and I've stopped in to tell you that the Board of Directors has voted Jeff Johnson out of office." Mark was awe-struck. "Not only that," Branch continued, "but I have been talking to the other Board members since that meeting and have their concurrence to invite you to a special board meeting next Wednesday, at which time you will be nominated to replace Johnson. Mark was surprised and pleased beyond words.

At the special Board meeting on Wednesday, the Vice-Chairman said, "Let's come to order. As a result of our last meeting, Jeff Johnson no longer works for the company, is no longer a member of this board and, therefore, is not in attendance today. I have invited Mark Hefron, Vice President of Finance for TTT to attend this special board meeting in his place and, at this time, I will entertain a motion to nominate Mark for the position of President and CEO of TTT.

"So motioned," said Fester Palmer.
"Do I hear a second?"
"I'll second," Conrad Enders said.
Branch then called for a vote. "All in favor." All but two hands went up. "Let the record show that the motion was carried by a majority. Mark, congratulations. It looks like you are going to be our new boss." Everyone in turn rose walked around the table and shook Mark's hand, adding their personal congratulation to his good fortune. Even Bess Flowers and Sherwood Henson joined in the parade. Flowers and Enders were both quick to inform Mark that although they were in favor of Jeff Johnson staying in office, Mark could count one hundred percent on their support now that the decision had been made. Yeah, Right, Mark thought.

Although it would be necessary for the stockholders to officially vote Mark into office at the next annual meeting, it was pretty much a formality and for all practical purposes, Mark was the new President and CEO. Branch said, "Mark, would you like to say a few words?"

"Thanks Ben, I would. Standing, he said, "I am honored to be chosen to replace Johnson. I think his replacement is way past due and I will do everything in my power to do a better job. For starters, I will listen to the technical leaders in the company and prevent the kind of problem that we have just gone through. I also promise that I will be responsive to the advice, counsel and concerns of this board. I thank you all."

CHAPTER THIRTY

While the TTT Board of Directors was voting Johnson out of office, Sara, in Rochester, was working frantically to get things organized so she could leave at 1:30 to be sure to arrive in Baldwinsville on time for her 3:00 pm meeting with Ethan Williams. She called her staff in to give her managers some last minute assignments before leaving.

"I anticipate being gone a couple of days," she told them, "Three at the most. There are a few things I'd like you to do while I'm gone."

"Charles," she said, to the middle aged man with gray wavy hair sitting across the table, "I want you to call Admiral Hopkins. Since his people were present, get his view on the burn-in test failures we witnessed at the IC supplier in San Jose yesterday. Summarize the results of your conversation in a report that I can edit as soon as I get back. I need to send it over to Bert."

"You know, Sara, I think those failures were a result of device design. If that's the case, and the supplier has to do a re-design, it'll mean program delay, which the Admiral won't like. Should I be up front and tell him what I think?"

"Absolutely. If that's the problem, let's find out and get at fixing it. The longer we wait, the worse it will be. Make sure the Admiral gets that message and let's work with the supplier to resolve the issue as fast as possible."

"Clayt, I want you to have one of your people call all of our ceramic suppliers and make sure they're on top of the latest Military Specification change on surface finish."

"You want me to call Cercon, too? They're the ones we told you about failing incoming inspection on the last two orders, and at our last Program review, we talked about dropping them as a supplier."

"I remember. Let's talk to them, too, since we haven't actually dropped them yet. If you think they understand what the change is all about, and are taking the proper action, then talk to them about giving them one more chance to ship us an acceptable batch of material. Make them understand that this will be their last chance to remain one of our suppliers."

"Okay. Can I tell them when they might expect another order?"

"No, not yet," she said, shifting her attention to the last person at the table.

"Judith, I'd like you to talk to Rudy Anderson at Averill Instruments about the corporate discount he and I discussed. He indicated there might be a threshold after which additional purchases would be eligible for a discount. See where he stands. Try to find out the break point and what kind of discount he's talking.

I'd like all of you to work the radar proposal inputs so I can review a final draft when I get back," Sara said. If anyone needs to reach me, see Susan. She'll know how to get in touch with me."

As soon as the office was clear, Sara called Susan in and said, "Susan, I'll be driving until three and will be in a meeting after that where I don't want to be disturbed. So if you want to reach me, leave a message on my cell. If it's after three and is an emergency, you can reach me in the meeting." She gave her Ethan's number and told her again to use it only in case of an emergency and if she didn't answer her cell phone.

Sara wove her way south to the New York State Thruway in the white BMW she had chosen as her company car. She took a route that encountered as few signal lights as possible to save time.

The company had purchased an E-Z Pass from the Thruway Authority that saved time. It allowed entrance and exit of the thruway by slowing down instead of stopping, and no fooling with money. Depositing money with the Thruway Authority, which was debited by a computer-controlled transmitter-receiver system, made payment: the transmitter was on the car windshield, and the receiver was at the tollbooth.

Once on the road, her trip started out easily. Then she ran into the construction. They were working on the shoulders, and putting down new blacktop. A trip that should have taken forty-five minutes took over an hour.

Sara hadn't been to Baldwinsville before and found it a nice little village. She located the PI's office, approached the door, knocked, and stepped inside.

Kavichi, still parked across the street, saw the woman arrive at Ethan's office. Based on how long it took to drive from Rochester and the time when Sara had called Williams, coupled with the fact that she was driving a Mercedes, Kavichi knew it had to be Sara. He would wait until she left and grab her someplace away from William's office.

"Ms. Stone, come in and have a seat," Ethan said, "it's nice to see you." As they shook hands, Sara said,

"It's nice to see you, too, Mr. Williams."
"Would you like coffee or a soda?"
"Yes. Coffee with nothing in it."
While walking across the office for the coffee, Ethan said, "Your brothers and sister should be here any minute." As he handed her the cup, he added, "Charles Boynton, the attorney for your father's estate, is also coming." And just as Ethan finished the sentence, the door opened, and the other three Farnsworth heirs entered the office. Sara was amused at how different her siblings looked. One was fat, one was plump, and one was well built. She compared them to herself, smiled, and wondered which of them had taken after their father.

When Kavichi saw the other three Farnsworth's arrive later and noted that the woman with them was not driving a

Mercedes, he knew for sure that the first woman who had arrived a few moments earlier was Sara.

CHAPTER THIRTY-ONE

Joyce, Harold, and George sat down at the conference table across from Ethan and Sara.

Ethan stood and said, "Sara, I'd like you to meet your sister Joyce." Joyce shook her hand.

"Also, I'd like you to meet your brothers, George and Harold." They both shook Sara's hand telling her that they were glad to meet her, also.

"I'm glad to meet all of you, too," Sara said, smiling.

Introduction formalities over, Ethan said, "Since we need Charles to conduct any formal business, I suggest the four of you use the time while we wait for him to arrive to get acquainted. There's coffee over there in the corner, and sodas in the refrigerator alongside the coffee. I'll be over here at my desk, Harold, if you need me. Ethan went to his desk and placed a call to make sure Charles Boynton was on his way.

Harold said, "Sara, we really are glad to meet you. We had no idea you existed until a few months ago when our father made the disclosure on his death bed."

"That makes me feel good – like I didn't exist?" Sara said facetiously.

"I grant you, Sara that our father did not do right by you. As he explained it to me, it was partly your mother's fault, too. Anyway, he was very serious about making things right by you. He specified in his Will that you are to inherit equally. Further, the rest of us could not inherit until we found you."

"Hoorah," Sara said with pursed lips.

"Don't be too hard on him, Sara. At least he did repent. You've heard the expression, 'Too little too late?' It may be a lot late, but believe me; it's not too little. I'll let Charles explain how much."

Joyce spoke up. "Sara, you can't imagine how pleased I am to have a sister. I'm only sorry we couldn't have known each other when we were growing up."

"I'm glad to have a sister, too," George added.

"Thank you all. I've tried all my life to find out from my mother about my father. She would never give me any information. I'm glad to meet you all, and very happy to finally have and know my family. I'm anxiously looking forward to hearing everything you'll tell me about our father." The door opened and Boynton came in. Harold stood up. "Charles I'd like you to meet our sister, Sara Stone."

"I'm pleased to meet you, Sara. You've given us a run for our money. And you've arrived just in time, as I have a date for us to appear in probate court next Wednesday at 10:00 am."

"How do you do, Charles? I'm sorry about making it hard for you to find me, but I had my reasons."

"Now that we're all together, let's get on with the business of Philip's Will," Boynton said, as he gave each of them a package of paper, and asked Harold to read the Will for Sara's benefit. After Harold finished, Charles took over again.

"I won't go over every detail, because you can find it in the package I just gave you. I will say, however, that the total estate is worth just over $28,000,000. Harold and I have each made an evaluation, and I had two independent assessments made. The minimum of the four is 28.2 and the maximum, 28.5. Here are the rules concerning taxes and distribution. After all debts are settled for the estate, including fees for the executor and me, the value of the inheritance will be established. That will occur before taxes and be established at probate. Taxes of fifty percent will be set-aside on the Estate. We have to submit a payment to the IRS within nine months and pay the balance within a year. In the meantime, the law allows our firm to make a payment to the heirs.

Here's what I've decided. I'll hold $14,000,000 for the IRS and allow half of what's left to go to you heirs immediately. Therefore, assuming everything goes according to plan, I'll issue a check to each of you next Friday for about $2,000,000. Does anyone have questions?" No one spoke so Boynton said, "Everyone will have to be at the court house next Wednesday at 8:30 am.

Now, I have an appointment at 4.30 so I have to leave and I'll see you then." He picked up his briefcase and left.

Finally, to break the silence, Harold said, "Let's have a cup of coffee." Ethan said, "I'll buy," getting up and heading for the coffee pot. While Ethan was getting the coffee, which Sara declined, Harold said, "I would like everyone to come over to my house this evening for dinner. It will give Sara a chance to meet Becky, Linda and John. They're our spouses, Sara. How does 8:00 sound?" Every one agreed that the time was okay and while they had their coffee, Harold drew a small map, showing Sara how to get from her hotel to his house and wrote his telephone number on the map. Leaving, Harold and Joyce headed for home, George for his office, and Sara to the diner she had passed on her way to Ethan's office. She wanted to sit down with a cup of tea and settle her nerves before going to her hotel where she would shower and rest a little before going to Harold's house for dinner. Entering the diner, she saw that it was decorated in a 1950's motif. She noticed the sign saying they had been in business for fifty years and were open 24 hours. The aroma was enticing; the smell of coffee mixed with French fries, soup and roast beef. Good thing she was going to Harold's for dinner or she would be tempted to eat. The place was crowded, so since she didn't have much time, rather than wait for a booth, she took a place at the counter and ordered the tea.

The diner was reminiscent of her college days when she either took her lunch or found places to eat that were cheap. A diner was always a place to get fairly good food at a low price. You usually knew what to expect, and good or bad, there were seldom any surprises.

The waitress came and asked her if she wanted seconds, bringing her thoughts back to the present. Sara looked at the clock on the wall at the end of the counter and realized that her time was getting short. She turned down the second cup of tea and asked for a check. As the waitress was leaving, Sara pulled a tip from her purse, put it on the counter, and went to the cashier to pay.

Outside, she headed for her car thinking about the upcoming dinner meeting with her siblings and their spouses. She was a little nervous. She would be much more comfortable heading for a boardroom and a group of executives. What would her brothers' and sister's spouses be like? Would she like them? Would they be hostile towards her or would they be friendly? How would she act? She wasn't sure, but she would finally get some answers about her family, answers that her mother had refused to give her for over twenty-five years; somehow, it didn't seem to have the same importance that it once had.

CHAPTER THIRTY-TWO

The man's dark-blue Ford four-door sedan was parked next to Sara's car and was facing in the opposite direction. She had no reason to pay any attention to it because she had used her remote control to unlock the door of her own car while crossing the parking lot. Sara opened the door, tossed her purse in, and had her right leg almost in the car when she heard the click of a door opening. She started to turn towards the noise, but before making a quarter turn, was embraced in a bear hug from behind, and felt a damp hand clamp over her mouth. Sara recognized the acrid smell of ether from her organic chemistry days in college, and everything started to spin. She jerked and twisted, wanting to scream, but was overcome with a feeling of euphoria just before everything went black.

The man holding her closed the front door of her car and opened the rear door of his. He quickly eased Sara into his backseat. He climbed in with her, tied her hands behind her back, tied her feet together, and put duct tape over her mouth. He exited the back seat, got into the front, and quickly left the parking lot heading east.

Sara woke up, felt her constraints, the tape over her mouth, and the car moving. It took a few moments for her to clear her head and remember what had happened. She struggled against her bonds to no avail. She wiggled her way around until her feet were off the seat. Then raising her shoulders and using her hands, pushed herself upright. Looking out the window, she could tell from the looks of the buildings, that she was in a city environment; not downtown, but in an area where there were apartment buildings opening onto sidewalks, neighborhood bars, restaurants, and stores. She had no idea where she was. The man driving the car turned part way around and said, "Welcome back, Beautiful." Sara mumbled and continued to strain against the ropes. As she wiggled and squirmed, she caught a glimpse of a street sign. "Shit," she muttered, as the street sign flew by without her being able to read it. Then the car pulled up to the curb and stopped.

The building they had stopped in front of was a dirty red brick with three steps from the sidewalk up to a door with a finish that was cracking and peeling. There was a dirty, bare window to the right of the door. The driver looked around the car carefully to make sure no one was in sight before getting out. He opened the back door and reached for Sara's legs. She kicked him. "Damn you!" he said, grabbing both her legs in one hand and untying them with the other. He pulled her out of the car, telling her if she behaved herself she wouldn't get hurt, then he half dragged her while she half walked to the door which he unlocked while pulling her inside. The room was empty except for a couch that was dirty and torn in several places with cotton sticking out of the tears. A small coffee table sat in front of the couch, and an end table at the end. Both tables were covered with empty and half empty coffee cups and each had an ashtray that was overflowing with cigarette butts. A roll-up type blind at the dirty window was rolled all the way down letting very little light through.

Sara's kidnapper took her through the front room that was apparently meant to be a living room, and then into a kitchen. Cleanliness-wise, it was worse than the room from which they had just come. The sink, what little could be seen of it under and around the Styrofoam, cardboard, and plastic containers, was filthy. The stove, refrigerator, and cabinets matched it in their accumulation of caked-on dirt. There was a door to their left, as they entered the kitchen. The man opened it and pulled Sara after him as he started down a pair of stairs. They were narrow, steep, and dark.

"Watch your step, Sweetie. I don't want you to hurt yourself." She gave him a kick. He let loose of her and started to fall but caught himself with the banister and immediately grabbed her wrists again saying, "You try something like that again, Sister, and you're going to get a fist to the jaw. Now come on," he said, as he grabbed her wrists and pulled her the rest of the way down the stairs behind him.

He yanked her through another door into a room in the basement that had no windows. The only source of light was a 60-watt bulb in a porcelain socket on the ceiling with a pull cord hanging from it. There was a table and one chair under the light. He untied her hands and forced her to sit, while ripping the tape from her mouth. Before she had a chance to say anything, he left locking the door behind him.

The size of the room reminded Sara of the one she had when she was living at home and going to school. Now she knows how good she had it. Her room, though small, was bright, clean, and smelled fresh. This room was without windows, cold, damp, and smelled like mildew. The single 60-watt incandescent bulb over the table cast eerie shadows. The room had a concrete floor and a cot in one corner, which had no mattress or blankets on it - just the canvas of a typical army-type cot. In the opposite corner was a dirty toilet and sink. What a disgusting place.

After the man left the room, she pounded on the door, looked for ways to escape, and screamed until she was hoarse. It did no good. Two hours later when he returned with something to eat, Sara asked why he had kidnapped her and brought her there. He said nothing.

According to her watch, that was four hours ago, and still she had no idea what was going on. Her first thought was Jeff Johnson. But why? To what avail? He wouldn't be that stupid even if he had something to gain, and she could think of nothing. Could it have something to do with his lawsuit or with her inheritance? Unlikely, she thought, though the latter made some sense, considering the magnitude of the inheritance. If someone had ransom in mind, who would pay it? That all seemed academic to her right now. The important thing was what to do.

He came in again, this time with a pillow and a blanket in his arms. "What am I doing here?" she demanded.

"That don't matter. Behave yourself and you'll be okay."

"Who are you?" she asked as she stood.

"You don't need to know that. Don't gimme any trouble and you'll find out soon enough. He threw the pillow and blanket to her, picked up some trash from the table and left. She heard the key turn in the lock. "Shit," she said throwing the blanket and pillow on the cot. Sara sat down at the table to try to think of a solution to her problem.

CHAPTER THIRTY-THREE

George was sitting at his desk when the telephone rang. He grabbed it and said, "Hello."

"Farnsworth, I've got your sister."

"What are you talking about, who the hell is this?"

"You heard me, I've got Sara, and I'm your worst nightmare."

"What the hell are you talking about?" George asked again, as he stood and started to pace. His mind was racing.

"So, Farnsworth, you want Sara out of the way?"

Oh no, he thought. Not now that I've finally started to turn my life around. What am I going to do?

"I called that off," George said in a panic, his eyes glazing over with tears, and his hands shaking.

"So you think, but not with me. To cancel with me, it'll cost you 250 Grand."

Thinking how hard he had worked in the last two months to get his drinking under control, gave him renewed strength and he said, "You're crazy, I don't have that kind of money."

"Look, Farnsworth, I did my homework. I know your old man was worth plenty, so don't tell me you don't have it."

"The Will hasn't been settled yet."

"That's your problem. I'll tell you the rules of this game. I want my money in two weeks. If not, I tell your brother and sister what you've done, and that they have to get the money."

"You can't do that," George countered.

"Oh, yeah? Watch me, and if they don't come up with the dough, your sister is history. I'll give you two days to figure out how you're gonna get the money, and then I'll call you again." The telephone went dead. George laid his head on the desk; he was scared and didn't know what to do. His drunkenness had led him to do an unthinkable thing. He had recanted, stopped drinking, and thought he had corrected what he had started. Now he finds out he hadn't. He let Secontini keep the deposit and, Secontini, true to his word, put out the order to cancel the hit. The problem was that the Hit Man decided to continue on his own agenda. Secontini had given him all the pertinent information, so instead of backing off as ordered, he decided to change the plan to his advantage. If things worked out the way he planned, he would be able to let Sara go and walk away rich.

George couldn't let Joyce and Harold find out what he had done. What would he tell them? There was no way he could explain the unexplainable no matter how sorry he was. George knew he would probably have the money within two weeks if Boynton followed through as he promised. The money was not the issue; Sara's welfare was, because he didn't trust the guy he had just talked to. After a few minutes he said, "God, what have I done?" He took a deep breath, leaned back in his chair, exhaled, and thought about what he should do. He reached over to the desk, picked up the telephone, and called Secontini.

"Secontini, this is George Farnsworth. I thought you called off the contract."

"I told you I called it off, and when I say I did something, I damn well mean it! I'm a man of my word! Now, what the hell is this all about?"

Well, I just got a call from someone who said he has Sara and was going to kill her if I didn't give him $250,000. He gave me two days to figure out how I'm going to get the money. You've got to help me. You have to call this guy off."

"Calm down, Farnsworth. There must be some kind of mix-up. Let me look into it."

"Okay! But be quick about it, because she is supposed to be in a meeting with my brother, my sister and me at 8:00. If we don't get this thing squared away fast, the heat's going to come down hard on all of us!"

"All right, relax, I'll get right on it." Secontini replied. He disconnected and immediately placed another call. "Kavichi, this is Secontini. I just heard you grabbed the Stone dame. I told you that job was off!"

"I know, I'm not gonna hurt her, I just thought I'd pick up a few bucks and let her go."

"You son of a bitch, you call 250 Grand a few bucks? You let her go right now, or you're going to be wearing a pair of concrete boots at the bottom of Onondaga Lake, you bastard. Do you understand? You're messing with my credibility!"

"Yeah, Orlando, I'll take care of it right away, and I'm sorry I didn't mean to cause you no trouble."

George and Linda were the first to arrive at Harold's house followed closely by Joyce and John. They sat around sipping coffee and making small talk. Finally John said, "I thought dinner was supposed to be at 8:00."

"It was," Becky answered, not too happy that her first dinner party with her new sister-in-law was going to be a disaster.

"Maybe she ran into a problem or got lost," Linda said.

"She could've called," her sister-in-law replied, starting to get mad.

Harold spoke up next. "Yeah, well, we'll wait a while longer."

George didn't say anything but was about to go mad wondering what was happening to Sara. Also, he was scared to death he was going to be exposed for the terrible act that he had committed. He took a deep breath and prayed that she was okay. Then he said, "Harold, why don't you call her hotel and see if they know anything."

"Harold, it is 8:45 and my roast won't wait any longer!" Becky insisted. "We have to eat!" She stomped off to the kitchen in tears. Harold went after her and said,

"Honey, don't cry, it's not your fault. I'll call the hotel while you put things on the table. We will have to eat without her, but at least I'll try to find out if something happened to her." George overheard him and shuddered.

Becky served the golden pork roast and Linda followed with the sweet potatoes. Joyce brought in the mashed potatoes and green beans. George, trying to get his mind off what might be happening to Sara, cut and served the hard-crust Italian bread. As Harold returned to the dining room from making his phone call, John stood and started to carve the roast.

They all sat down and Harold said, "The person at the hotel said he didn't know anything about the whereabouts of Sara. I asked to speak to the manager and the clerk said he went home at 6:00. So, I guess we will just have to wait until we hear from her. They all sat down and Harold said Grace before they started to eat.

Downtown in her basement cell, Sara was sitting at the table in the middle of the room staring at the door. As bad as things were, her captor did feed her, although it was fast food. As she stared at the door, she had a stark recollection.

She had recently read a novel by David Baldacci entitled *Last Man Standing*. In the book, a ten-year old son of a drug dealer was kidnapped and locked in a room much like Sara. The street-smart and intelligent boy removed the pins from the hinges of a door to escape. As she sat looking at the hinges, she wondered how she could do the same thing. The boy had taken the leg off a bench and used it to force the pins out. Sara, having a degree in engineering, had been interested in the trick. Now she rose

198

and went to examine the pins. They had a ball-like top with a necked down area just before the pin entered the hinge. It appeared that the necked down area was meant to be a place where an object such as the blade of a screwdriver could be placed to drive the pin upward and out of the hinge. Obviously, she didn't have a screwdriver. She started looking around. There wasn't much in the room. She examined the legs of the table and chair. Unlike the legs on the bench in the book she had read that screwed on, the legs on her table and chairs were bolted on. They could not be removed without a wrench. She went over to the toilet area. There was nothing.

Next, she walked over to the opposite corner where the sink was located. Behind it was a round hole in the floor. Sara walked around and looked in to find a small amount of water in the bottom. This was a sump pump hole. Sara had read about them, but this was the first one she had actually seen. She got down on her knees to examine it. She could see water but the hole was dark. She reached down into the water and found debris in the bottom. She felt around, and pulled out a piece of concrete. Reaching in again Sara pulled out a skinny piece of metal. It was a nail about three inches long. I'm in business, she thought.

CHAPTER THIRTY-FOUR

Taking the nail and the piece of concrete over to the door, she placed the point of the nail under the ball of the pin in the middle hinge, and swung at it, missing the nail completely. The jagged concrete hit her hand and drew blood. "Shit!" she exclaimed, as she dropped her makeshift hammer and the nail, quickly pulled her bleeding hand to her mouth.

After a moment, ignoring the blood, she picked up her tools and prepared for another try. This time, she held the nail closer to the end, was careful to get it exactly in the center of the pin, and tapped it. Three more tries and it dropped to the floor. The bottom one came out with less trouble, and to do the top one, it was necessary to get a chair to stand on. It was the hardest of the three to get out, but persistence prevailed, and it fell to the floor.

Sara stepped back and looked at the door. As in Baldacci's novel, when her captor opened the door it should fall inward pulling him with it. Then what? The chair could be used to hit him as he was pulled off balance by the door and through the entrance.

Sara went over and picked up the chair to feel its weight. She could handle it. Leaning her back against the wall, she held the chair by the back with her arms from right-to-left across her body and the seat of the chair to her left. It felt comfortable. Before she could move from her practice position, she heard footsteps outside. The key turned in the lock. The knob turned. The door came inward, and the man stumbled right behind it. Sara made her move. She brought the chair around and down on his head at the same time he and the door hit the floor. He just lay there. She raised the chair and hit him again to make sure he wouldn't get up. If it hadn't been aluminum, the chair would've been in splinters. Sara stood there trembling for a few moments. After her nerves settled, she rolled him over, unbuckled, and pulled off his belt, then rolled him back onto his face. With the belt, she tied his hands behind his back, took the bag he'd brought food in, wadded it up, and stuffed it into his mouth. Taking his handkerchief from his back pocket, she used it to secure the gag so he couldn't spit it out. Finally, she took her own belt and used it to bind his feet bringing the end up and tying it to the belt holding his hands.

She stepped back and examined her work. Satisfied, she sat down on the chair to give her nerves a chance to settle and collect her thoughts. Looking at her captor lying unconscious on the floor, Sara's mind was racing. She had many questions. Now that she was free, what was she going to do? She had missed the dinner party with Harold, George, and Joyce without explanation. What would she tell them? Being the pragmatic person that she was, she didn't want anyone to know what had just happened until she herself had some idea what it was all about. It was probably too late for anyone to call her office. If they did, how would she explain to them that she was unavailable? She could handle that, she thought. She didn't want to get involved with the police and a police report, because that would probably get the news media involved and create publicity, which would not be good for her or the company. Then she decided what she would do.

Just as she finished sorting out the plan in her mind, the man started to move. Sara took hold of his hair and lifting his head, said, "You piece of shit! I want to know who hired you and why you kidnapped me." He made muffled noises because of the gag. Sara, still holding onto his greasy hair, banged his head against the floor and said, "I'm going to take this gag out of your mouth, and I don't want any funny stuff or yelling, do you understand?" He didn't respond. She banged his head against the floor harder and said, "DO YOU UNDERSTAND?" He groaned in pain and nodded. "All right!" She unfastened the gag. "Now answer my question."

"I kidnapped you for the money. Nobody hired me. It was my idea and I was coming to release you."

"Why were you going to release me?"

"I can't say." She banged his head against the floor again.

"That won't help, lady. I'm not saying any more."

Sara replaced his gag and said, "You bastard, I'm leaving here and calling the police. I'm reporting you as a thief and rapist. I hope they put you away for life! If you ever get out, don't try to come after me. I've got my own security force that will be watching my back. You don't even want to think what they'll do to you if you screw around with me again. Do you understand?" He didn't respond. She kicked him in the ribs and yelled, "DO YOU UNDERSTAND?" He groaned in pain and nodded his head. "All right!" She left the room looking at her watch and seeing that it was 10:20 pm, she thought, oh, what am I going to tell Harold.

At the corner, Sara found a small market and a pay phone. She called Harold.

Sara, where have you been?"

You didn't get a message?" She replied, pretending that she had left a message for him. She apologized for missing their dinner party and explained that she had received a call from the president of one of their customer companies who demanded that she meet with him and an admiral. There was a major technical problem on a large and critical military program that had to have top-level management attention. Sara told Harold that she tried to talk the customer into letting her send someone else but he wouldn't even consider it. Since the meeting was scheduled to take place in Rochester and Sara had to be briefed as well as prepare for the meeting, it was impossible for her to call. She had left a message with a clerk at the hotel to ask the manager to call Harold, but apparently, for some reason, that hadn't happened. She told Harold that she would make it up to them and asked him to give everyone her apology. Especially Becky. She said in a way to start the make-up, she wanted to buy everyone breakfast the next morning and asked Harold for the best restaurant in the area for breakfast. He suggested the Holiday Inn on Ferrell Road and gave her directions. They set the time for 8:00 am and Harold said he would call Joyce and George. After calling a cab, Sara made a call to the police department to make an anonymous report about the thief and rapist tied up in the basement of the house on Salina Street. Not being able to get her name, they said they'd look into it.

When the cab arrived she told the driver she wanted to go to the diner in Baldwinsville. Sara found her car where she had left it. She couldn't believe it. The door was unlocked as she had left it and her purse was still on the front seat. What an honest village, she thought. Opening the door, she said, "Unbelievable," as she spotted the keys on the seat where she had dropped them when the kidnapper had grabbed her. She got in, started the car, and headed for her hotel on Route 31, took a shower and went to bed.

The next morning, Sara was rested and calm. She had gotten up very early to make sure she would be on time for her breakfast meeting. Now that her ordeal was all over, she was anxious to tell Mark about her good fortune. She had some time before breakfast, so she picked up the phone and called him. "Hi Mark, it's been a long time."

"Boy, that's for sure, I've been meaning to call you but have been so busy that I keep putting it off. You know how it is. I guess you have been busy, too, huh."

"I sure have. You remember that PI that was trying to find me?"

"Yeah, I presume you called him based on our last conversation."

"I did and I went to see him. Mark, you won't believe this, but I have inherited some money, a lot of money."

"How much is a lot?"

"Sit down and hold onto something."

"Is it that good?"

"I have inherited approximately seven million dollars."

"Holy mackerel, Sara, you're kidding"

"Nope, and I should get two million of it within a week."

"That is unreal," Mark said, as he laid his head back against the chair and closed his eyes, thinking, holy hell, my girlfriend is a millionaire. He said to Sara jokingly, "I have always wanted to be involved with a wealthy woman. You want to get married?"

"Now he wants to get married," she responded. "Seriously, Mark, I have no idea what to do with that kind of money. I plan to check with Merrill Lynch, some other investment houses and discuss the matter with Bert Levitt for his advice before I do anything."

"That sounds like a plan to me," Mark said. Then added, Sara, I am really happy for you. I don't know what else to say except ask who left you the money?"

"My father. Would you believe it? I have been trying to find out something, anything, about him all my life to no avail. Now, out of the blue he dumps a truckload of money on me. You know what makes me almost as happy as getting the money"

What?"

I found out that I have two half brothers and a half sister and they live in Syracuse only 45 minutes away from me."

"That is wonderful, Sara, and again, I am very happy for you."

"Well," Sara said, "in my excitement, I have been doing all the talking and haven't let you say anything. How are things going with you?"

"I can't begin to match your tale, though I do have some good news that I think you will like. The Board of Directors has voted Jeff Johnson out of office."

"That *is* good news, Mark," Sara said, interrupting him.

"That's only half of my news" he said, as he continued, excited and anxious to share his own good fortune with her. "The board has nominated me to replace him as President and Chief Executive Officer."

"Oh, Mark, that is absolutely wonderful," she said, wishing she were there so she could throw her arms around his neck, hold him close, and smother him in kisses. Her eyes got moist in her happiness for him. "It shows the board has more sense then I gave them credit for. They are just a little slow. I know you are the right man and will do an outstanding job. When will it be official, Mark?"

"The Annual Stock holder's Meeting takes place on the eighth of November in New York. My election will be the first item on the agenda. I would like you to be there with me."

"Nothing short of death could keep me away. Let's get together this weekend and celebrate," Sara said.

"You think we have enough to warrant it?" he asked.

"Yeah, and I'll swing for a bottle of champagne," she said, smiling."

"Shall we meet on the boat or someplace different?" Mark asked

"Since you haven't seen my place yet, I would like you to come here. You can either drive or fly and I'll pick you up at the airport. What do you think of that?"

"That sounds great and I'll fly because it will be faster. I should be able to get a plane out Friday afternoon. I'll call you tomorrow and let you know what time," he said. They said their good byes, hung up, and went back to work.

Earlier that week after the details of Philip Farnsworth's Will had been settled, and his lawyer and heirs had left the office, Ethan sat down at his desk and prepared the final bill for Harold. Sliding the computer keyboard out of the way, he placed his elbows on top of the desk, and rested his chin in his hands. Ethan closed his eyes and thought over the history of his fairly young business. Most of his cases had dealt with insurance fraud or missing persons. The insurance fraud cases were easy. He was always given the name of the suspect. Then, all he had to do was follow and watch the individual until he proved him innocent or guilty. He worked on time plus expenses until the job was done. There was always a distinct start and a distinct end. Those jobs he liked.

Missing persons cases, on the other hand, were different. Although the start was generally clear, the end could go either way. He had not encountered one like the Farnsworth case, though. In the beginning, he didn't know where to start. After he got started, it moved like molasses on a cold winter day. And then, it went in spurts, on again, off again, but seemed to go nowhere. There were times when he wondered if there was an end. Now that it was over, he was glad, and wished he still had Beth to share the moment with. In one of their philosophical discussions concerning marriage and the future, they had agreed that if something happened to one of them, the other should continue their life in a normal manner as soon as possible. Ethan's pain was gradually lessoning and the hole left in his heart by Beth's passing beginning to close. In keeping with their discussions, it was time for him to be appreciative of the inheritance she had left him and move on.

EPILOGUE

The Ethan Williams Private Investigations Company continued to prosper. Although Ethan remained in his office in Baldwinsville, he hired a secretary and added a second investigator to the payroll. His new associate, fifteen years his junior, brought computer skills to the firm that are essential in today's high-tech environment. The money he inherited from Beth was put into an account and used as a buffer when needed to keep things going between jobs.

George continues to attend AA meetings and stay in touch with his sponsor because occasionally he still gets the urge for a drink. He paid off all his debts, and invested the rest of his money with Shepard, Shane, and Barnes. He figured if they could do for him what they had done for his father, he and Linda would be quite happy. They worked together to improve their spending habits and George's sobriety worked wonders for the business.

Harold and Becky had twins, a boy and a girl. They named the boy Harold Ethan and the girl Becky Sara. They put one third of their inheritance into a trust for Becky, one third into a trust for Harold and kept the other third for themselves. They moved into a new house on the Seneca River that had three bedrooms, and relocated their bookstore to a larger space in the mall. Their business tripled and they kept most of their old customers. With his new responsibilities as a father and the clinical proof of the relationship of obesity to heart disease, Harold took on a serious diet and exercise program.

Joyce and John expanded their business. They added four new trucks a significant amount of new equipment, an office manager and a secretary for both the plumbing business and the heating business. They built a new office where John could oversee the total operation, and hired him a new secretary with the understanding that she was not allowed to chew gum.

TTT, under Mark's leadership, pulled out from under the stigma that Jeff Johnson had created and went on to become a world leader toy company. They championed child safety in toys and proved corporate citizenship by dedicating millions of dollars in cash and millions more in toys each year to research and development to achieve their safety goals.

Sara invested most of her money in Ramax and TTT. Both stocks were doing well. She excelled in her job with Ramax and found the company to meet her every expectation. She and Mark continued their weekend relationship with a great deal of pleasure and satisfaction.

Sara suggested they start their own company since money wasn't a problem. After much discussion, they concluded that there was too wide a gap between their interests of commercial and military technology, so in the end, decided to continue status quo and to deal with the distance issue. They did think, however, that it might be nice if Mark was on the Ramax Board of Directors and Sara was on the TTT Board of Directors. They agreed to work on that.

Charles Boynton and his firm were happy in that they were able to keep a significant amount of the Farnsworth money with the firm.

Kavichi was picked up by the police, booked, and put into jail. He asked for, and was assigned, a lawyer who succeeded in getting him released at arraignment based on a lack of evidence. He never bothered Sara nor did he ever work for Secontini again.